PLAY PRETTY BLUES

Robinsonville

Friars Point

Clarksdale

Tutwiler

Columbus

Greenwood

Quito

Belzoni

MISSISSIPPI

Yazoo

Meridian

Jackson

Hazlehurst

Martinsville

Pascagoula

Pass Christian

SNOWDEN WRIGHT

PLAY PRETTY BLUES

A NOVEL OF THE LIFE OF ROBERT JOHNSON

Engine Books
Indianapolis

Engine Books
PO Box 44167
Indianapolis, IN 46244
enginebooks.org

Also available in eBook formats from Engine Books.

Printed in the United States of America

10 9 8 7 6 5 4 3 2 1

ISBN: 978-1-938126-10-9

Library of Congress Control Number: 2013935829

PART ONE

"Honeymoon Blues"

The first time Robert Johnson died he wasn't Robert Johnson. On a dog day in the summer of 1928, as then heard by two of us and as later verified in newsprint by all six of us, a man fitting his description walked into the Sparks Farm Cotton Gin five minutes before it was demolished by dynamite. The man who walked in the front door was called Robert Spencer. The man who snuck out the back door named himself Robert Johnson.

We have spent the past seventy years searching for him. Time and again, he has evaded our pursuit. Time and again, he has given us but sight of his ghost. We have questioned locals and stapled signs to phone poles. We have thumbed through classifieds and whittled cryptic on bathroom walls. We have dry-rubbed headstones, placed wires statewide, and notified the sheriff. We have caught glimmer of his coattails, found footprints in red mud, and heard his laugh peal from a passing sedan. We have convinced ourselves he'll send word. We have lied to his children. His name may not be the same to all of us—Mary Sue called him Caruthers, Betty called him Ledbetter—but to all of us he was husband.

Although they are by no means exhaustive, our records indicate that he was born the tenth child in a family known as Dodds, that he would eventually assume twelve separate aliases, that he officially died at least eight different times. The deaths were as fierce as his talent. In 1932, he was found straddling the bowl in an Arkansas white man's outhouse, his face dismantled by the business end of a twelve-gauge. In 1929, somewhere between Memphis and Olive Branch, he turned a stolen Model T the wrong way on a one-way street. In 1936, he was discovered on the tracks behind a railway juke joint, his head set free of its soulless coil by a Louisiana-bound locomotive. Between 1933 and 1935, he was thrice buried in graves whose stones bore only two chiseled lines, one intersecting the other, that many believe symbolized our heavenly father's time on the cross but that we maintain, even to this day, stood for the Roman numeral representing the place our children's father held in the lineage of his family. His guitar, as he explained to each of us in post-coital sheets, bore that very mark for that very reason. "Momma sees it from above," he said, sweat dripping on the strings. "I know it in my fingertips."

The last time he died would last a lifetime. It would linger seventy years beyond the date, August 13, 1938, the evening of which he played at a country dance near Greenwood, Mississippi. It would echo in the shucked chambers of our chests as we lived through wars abroad and at home, through bondage, oppression, and freedom, through poverty and wealth of kith and kin. That at the time of his death he was less than thirty miles from each of our homes, that he mentioned to more than one passerby he meant to "return to his true family," would perpetuate forever our questions that will go, as we now suspect, forever unanswered. *Did he love us?* we ask ourselves to this day. *Did we love him?*

All we can truly know is how we felt upon hearing the details of his final performance on this earth. At the country dance outside Greenwood, Robert Johnson, husband, father, legend, stood on a sawdust-covered stage, located the most attractive woman in the audience, and played his songs in her direction; he sang lyrics drenched with innuendo and made eye contact that could blind the weak, all methods we know first-hand. The explanation of his death confirmed most often by townsfolk from that evening involves the husband of the woman at whom he aimed his blues seduction. The husband sought vengeance by lacing the suspect bluesman's whiskey with strychnine.

We knew the exact moment the poison entered his bloodstream. Helena wrung her tablecloths bloody. Mary Sue dreamt twisted visions of God's wrath. Claudette spiced her cornbread with tears. Betty shook the cradle with her wails. Each of us saw the same vision of our husband crawling on the ground, hands and knees minced to ribbons by gravel, bottle tops, and cockleburs. Each of us watched in our minds as the toxin seeped into our husband's brain, causing him to howl and to froth like a dog gone rabid. His limbs contorted in all the wrong ways. His eyes searched heavenward though his face looked elsewhere. At last, somewhere in a cotton field on a sleepy Delta dawn, Robert Johnson collapsed to the ground, dead.

Each of us lived at least half a day from the fateful scene. On the night of his murder, according to the stories that reached us by week's end, a handful of drunks managed to form a search party, but their determination proved inversely proportional to their sobriety. They dropped their torches at first light. They called it a day on principle. Most of them left in pursuit of more whiskey, while the rest returned to their homes and families. Somewhere in a cotton field outside Greenwood, Mississippi, the body of our husband lay rotting beneath the highest stalks in county history. It was never found.

We will forever ponder his accidental grave. Did the hounds not track his scent because they smelled one of their own? Is there such thing as sacred ground for a man without a soul? Did his dark skin blend into the pitch of Precambrian floodplain?

Nary a public bulletin heralded the death of the musician who would one day be called the greatest blues singer of all time. The papers issued not a single proclamation. The wireless broadcast not a single eulogium. They should have waxed sensational on his genius in the newborn art; they should have poeticized his mastery of truss rod and fret board; they should have decreed music's end come nigh. In the weeks following his death, none of those who attended Robert Johnson's last performance reported the incident to the media or to authorities. The perpetrator of the crime, whose guilt we still deem beyond doubt, was never sentenced to his rightful acreage in Parchman Farm. We were deprived the sweet clink of shackle and chain, the lovely still-life of his face behind bars, the elegiac spectacle of his incarceration. Only time would avenge our husband's murder.

Since his death our lives have been guided not merely by our search for the truth but also by our desire for retribution. We have lived in the shadow of a ghost. In the first few years after his demise, some of us migrated north to St. Louis and Chicago, some of us west to Texas and Oklahoma, all in trace of the path taken by his posthumous musical influence. Claudette collected a dossier of evidence of his life and death, including fingerprints, oral accounts, facial sketches, Mason jars of sampled soil, photographs and lithographs and phonographs, vials, beakers, bottles, locks of hair hermetically sealed in Tupperware and Glad-Lock. Mary Sue, the oldest of us, seduced every headliner she heard cover a Robert Johnson song. Tabitha, the youngest, spent years harassing his murderer's family with coins glued to their porch's floorboards, caps twisted loose on their salt shakers, and staples removed from their Swingline. Betty sought solace in the bottle. Helena, who never forgave herself for not bearing our mutual husband an heir, eventually married a writer of crossword puzzles and gave birth to three boys named various anagrams of "Robert Johnson."

Even though we firmly believed in his death, our lives were plagued by the possibility he may still be among us. We raided whorehouses and drug dens in the hope we might find him astride a jaybird harlot. We saw eidetic echoes of his face in our compacts. We tore the feathered phone numbers from flyers for guitar lessons, staked-out record companies, deciphered liner notes, and showed up for open-call auditions, always expecting to find him as the sinister mastermind behind the music. We berated look-a-likes on the street, yanking on their hair that had to be a wig, tugging at their noses that had to be prosthetic. We opened our mailboxes looking for postcards from some Pacific archipelago or letters with lines blacked-out by some bureaucratic censor.

Only after we had given up hope of his return, only after we allowed ourselves to believe he was dead and would remain so forever, was Robert Johnson finally resurrected by music critics, record executives, and sales charts. It all began in 1961. Rock and roll musicians discovered his newly released LPs and scrutinized his techniques on the Gibson. Historians researched his life and investigated his death. Reporters held the public rapt with the story of his bargain at the crossroads. Decades after his death, our husband was famous to all the world, and we wept with both joy and sorrow. No longer were we the sole bearers of his memory. No longer was he ours and ours alone.

CHAPTER ONE

On the morning before Robert Johnson's conception, his mother, Julia Major Dodds, stirred a cast-iron kettle over an open flame in the kitchen of the cracker farmhouse she shared with her husband, five daughters, and four sons. She scraped muddled honeysuckle from a mortar and pestle into the concoction simmering over the woodstove. From the pantry she removed a small jar of myrtleberry oil imported by way of Hannibal, and from the cabinet she removed a roughhewn bag of locust essence cinched tight with cotton-bale twine. She added a pinch and a drop to the pot and stirred it with an oaken ladle.

Julia Dodds was a jook doctor. Any ailment suffered by the sharecropper population within twenty miles of Hazlehurst, Mississippi, home to the Dodds family and perhaps a dozen other black landowners, could be cured at the gentle, expert hands of Miss Julia. Her serums and tonics could rectify a tummy ache, the shivers, the shakes, head pains, back pains, neck pains, double vision, cottonmouth, poor taste, poor smell, hangover, and pregnancy. Her tinctures and balms could treat a copperhead bite, a mud-dauber sting, the spray of a skunk, barbed-wire gashes, briar-patch punctures, tooth rot, foot rot, crotch rot, and all manner of rash and hive. At least twice daily a hurt or ill fieldworker would knock on her door in need of remedy. Miss Julia's years of training with her great-grandmother, a medicine woman from West Africa prone to tribal gyrations and ancestral lingo—the term "jook," which would later be bastardized as "juke" to describe many of the venues our husband played, meant in the mother tongue "disorderly" or "infamous"—were augmented by a short apprenticeship with an apothecary on Magazine Street in New Orleans.

"What's cooking this morning?" asked her husband, Charles. He engaged his forearm around Julia's waist and with his lips explored the soft skin of her neck and shoulder. "Something sweet, I see. Taste like honey."

"That ass-ugly Collier boy got the worms in his feet."

"Now why you got to get all lovey-dovey with your talk?" Charles took grasp of his wife's substantial thighs. "Here I am about to go to work, and you got to get all lovey-dovey with your talk. 'That ass-ugly Collier boy,' she says. 'Worms in his feet,' she says."

Owner of a hundred acres of buckshot farmland, purveyor of homespun wicker furniture, and counsel to various overseers in Hazlehurst's outlying townships, Charles Dodds Jr. was as respected in the community as he was adored by Julia. They had been married twenty-one years. Charles's interactions with his wife—her collection of journals, lyrical and poetic and lovely, has proven invaluable for detail—were similar to our interactions with their son. Both men loved for love's sake. Both men were not without a sense of obligation. Both men romanticized their romanticism. They could never tolerate silence in their lives. They would always whisper the God's honest.

"You are the only woman I could ever give my heart,"

Charles said aft of his wife's ear. It was his daily incantation. "Don't you forget them words."

"Haven't yet."

"Me either."

"Breakfast?"

"Got no time. Mister Marchetti said he wants his chairs delivered first thing. Have to do it myself or it won't get done. Don't wait up for me tonight."

Charles made his way to the barn as Julia continued tending her poultice. Although the month of September was in its descendant, days still reached high into the nineties and nights offered little if any relief. The approaching fall would be an Indian summer. Charles grew flush with exertion and wet with perspiration as he placed three wicker chairs, one wicker table, two wicker footstools, and one wicker chaise onto the wagon bed. Each piece was his own special design. He would soak hundreds of cornhusks in sealed vats of dye and weave the husks throughout the furniture's crosshatch of reeds and cane, creating complex patterns with variegated shades of red, green, yellow, and blue. A Choctaw tribesman had taught him the technique during the tobacco hornworm outbreak of 1895.

Charles hitched the harness and stowed a saddlebag. He palmed the reins and nickered the horses. At the start of his trip, a trail of crimson dirt in front, a sheet of overcast above, a hill of shaggy pasturage on either side, Charles resituated his position atop the wagon seat in order to glimpse his home fading in perspective. We can imagine his thoughts. He mentally prioritized the necessary house repairs between the most urgent and the least, including the weathervane that had bent in last month's high winds and the clothesline wire that had snapped in this month's high heat. He decided to stake an area of the backyard for a sunflower garden. He planned to fertilize the vegetable patch by Christmas. He hoped with all of his being, as he studied a wisp of smoke seeping from the clinker-brick chimney on the tin roof, as he watched his wife in stark relief crossing the dogtrot of their clapboard farmhouse, he hoped on his life he would be able to stay true to the solemn vows he'd made to Julia on the day of their nuptials. He also resolved to fix the slop bucket in the livestock corral.

The Tallyho Plantation, 12,000 acres of cotton farmland and pine forest owned by the Marchetti family, lay in the northwest corner of Copiah County. The trip took Charles four hours. On a hummock of fertile soil, the house seat of the plantation was situated facing eastward, its back turned on a tupelo cypress gum brake in the dale below. Every member of the Marchetti family lived in a Greek revival mansion with pale Corinthian columns, and every servant of the household lived in a cluster of ramshackle tenants hidden way back in the marshy woods. Charles brought his wagon to a halt at the livery stable, knocked on the back door of the main house, removed his slouch hat from his sweaty mop, and waited with his hands crossed at the button of his breeches. A houseboy Charles had never met opened the door. One of the young man's eyes looked to have been kicked by a mule.

"Which of the misters you want?"

"Mister Franklin."

"I'll get him. You stay waiting outside."

Charles promptly slipped into the kitchen when the houseboy was gone from sight. On a butcher block near the sink sat a plucked chicken and a bowl of cornmeal. A frying pan simmered on the stove. Around the foot of the icebox lay a carpet of feathers and down. Charles walked to a door that led into a long hallway, but he chose not to explore the house any further. It would be unnecessary. At the end of the hall on the right was an antechamber with a cut-glass chandelier overlooking a twin staircase. The second step from the bottom, Charles knew, creaked loud enough to wake a light sleeper. At the end of the hall on the left was a parlor with a velveteen couch sitting next to a grandfather clock. The pendulum encased in mahogany, Charles knew, chimed the turn of an hour four minutes fast.

"What you doing in here?" the houseboy with the misshapen eye said from the door on the other side of the kitchen. "Thought I told you to keep yourself outside."

"I know, but the—"

"Never you mind the matter. Mister Franklin's on the front porch, wants to talk with you. No, no. Go back outside and walk *around* the house."

According to townsfolk who knew him, Franklin Marchetti, younger brother of Anthony Jr. and Terrence, youngest son of Anthony Sr. and Bettina, stood five-foot-four in Jodhpur boots and weighed a hundred twenty pounds after a big lunch. He waxed his moustache with Hungarian pomade made special by his mother. His defining characteristic was a comical propensity to grab his sex during moments of confusion or pride. He was famous for his wit, which was all but nonexistent. On the afternoon of Charles's delivery, Franklin suffered through the heat by putting himself in position to take the breeze, even lighting a special blend of cigar his oldest brother claimed mitigated overactive sweat glands. Charles waited in the front yard 'til he was invited onto the porch. Days later, we know from his official statement made to the county sheriff, Franklin Marchetti would be surprisingly forthright about his conversation with Charles Dodds prior to the incident that evening.

"Come on up here, boy," Franklin said, his words visualized by syrupy tobacco smoke. "Heard you had a goodly yield on your place this year."

"We did all right this year, yessuh."

"Any conjectures on the next?"

"I got a feeling we'll have a dry spell in June, but we'll pull through what with July around the corner." The smoke tickled Charles's nostrils. "July'll be drippy."

"No droughts or floods in our days?"

Farmers only talk of bad fortune when times are good, and farmers only talk of good fortune when times are bad. 1910 was a good year. Franklin could not resist the urge to list all the possible disasters that might befall his cotton crop in the coming months. He mentioned every known disease: wet weather blight, nematodes, fusarium wilt, root rot, black arm, yellow arm, rust, spot blotch, the dread boll weevil. Charles refuted each one.

"You bring that renown Dodds wicker with you?"

"Yessuh. Back the wagon."

"I'll have my new nigger help you unload it."

"Thank you kindly."

It was at that moment the door to the front porch opened to reveal one of the Marchetti family's young servants, Mary Thorne. She wore a summer frock despite the time of year. Her face and figure were beautiful, delicate, and inevitable. She gave a childish impression of concurrent servility and defiance. On her departure from the porch, after she had refilled Franklin's sipping whiskey and after he had thanked her with a pat on the fanny, Mary Thorne caught Charles's gaze in her own, held it steady, and allowed him to wink at her. Charles didn't have to look in her eyes to know they were the color of chicory.

Julia Dodds spent the day making house. Along about eight in the morning, her children had emerged from their room, taken breakfast, and begun their daily chores on the farm. The two oldest rode to the commissary for fatback and sugar, the four middle children tended the lower twenty, and the three youngest scattered feed to the chickens and pigs. Julia shelled butter beans on the porch. She boiled coffee for red-eye gravy and retrieved a ham hock from the smokehouse. She scrubbed salt from the meat and let it simmer stovetop for hours. She doused hot biscuits with blackstrap molasses. Along about two in the afternoon, her children had eaten lunch on the picnic table in the backyard, collected their writing tablets, gathered their script utensils, and taken seats cross-legged in a circle around Julia on the porch. It was time for school.

During her own childhood, Julia had been given the alphabet by one Theodore Stahl, her mother's former owner, who professed the transformative powers of language, especially amongst the "mongrel races." That was why Julia was so steadfast in her children's education. That was also why her journals were such a find for us. On the afternoon in question, Julia taught her youngest arithmetic, her middle children grammar, and her oldest literature. She gave rewards for right answers. Bessie and Sally, fraternal twins, got dress patterns for "Setting means time and place both." Samuel got rose oil for "I before E except after C." Natalie, slow in the head and given of lenience, got gumdrops for "Two plus two equals yellow."

We have often wondered how a woman as clever as Julia Dodds could have not put together the truth about her husband. How could she have not seen through his sweet, sweet talk? Her twin daughters, Sally and Bessie, their older selves acquiescent to our questions, described her as oblivious, oblivious, oblivious. "Momma had no idea whatever," they told us, "not even after what happen." They were mistaken. Even though Julia most certainly suspected her husband, all of us have come to admit, she simply could not allow herself to act on those suspicions. Women always want to know, but women never want to believe.

On the fateful day in September of 1910, still and all, Julia was correct in believing her husband spent the afternoon unloading wicker furniture for the Marchetti family. He bore the chairs, table, footstools, and chaise from the wagon bed, carrying them through the house to the second-floor gallery. He took a shammy cloth to the wicker's film of red dust. He arranged each piece to provide the best ergonomic comfort without distracting from the overall aesthetic effect. The man with only one good eye helped Charles throughout the afternoon.

"What you call them colors?"

"I named this design 'Autumn Harvest.'"

"Hmmph."

Little is known of the man who'd been hired in August to look after the plantation's day-to-day. Born in McComb to a large family of field workers and raised on various plantations across the Pine Belt, the thirty-two-year-old was considered ruthless, authoritative, trustworthy, and discreet in his duties as one of the youngest overseers in Mississippi history. He was said to have lost the use of his eye when as a toddler he stood behind a molly in estrus. He was also said to have cost seven men the give in their kneecaps for speaking poorly of his appearance. The rumor mill has ground the rest of his biography into fictitious pulp. Some say he fought in the Spanish-American War as a "Weary Walker" under the command of Colonel Leonard Wood. Others say he died of tuberculosis at one of the few racially tolerant sanatoriums in New Mexico. Even the man's name, Noah Johnson, is thought by many to be an invention.

It was dusk by the time Charles and Noah were done with their work. They shook hands studying their feet. Noah went back to the house for his evening talk with the boss, and Charles guided his wagon along a trail that led to the post road. He parked in a wildflower thicket hidden from sight. Over the next two and a half hours, day giving into night, light giving into dark, Charles sat by himself on a seed bag in the wagon bed. He dealt solitaire with a Bicycle deck. He drew hangman doodles with a carpenter's pencil. At a quarter past nine, he lit a coal-oil lantern with his last match, put wheel chocks under the chassis, found a worn path in the brush, and made his way towards the servant quarters. The Marchetti family should have been done with dinner.

Mary Thorne lived in a shotgun house on the brink of a foggy slough. In the front yard, a copse of bottle trees, whose purpose, according to West African tradition, was to ward evil spirits, caught the moonlight. The glass of the bottles cast green and brown flickers on the ground whilst chiming a soft melody all throughout the deep woods. In the backyard, an army of chorus frogs sang for mates within the vicinity, each note of their call euphonized by the creak of longleaf pine. Charles knocked on the door.

"Welcome home, soldier." Mary Thorne stood in the entry with one hand resting on her hip. "Beginning to think you wouldn't make it tonight."

"I didn't know how long you'd be serving dinner."

"They finished early."

"Lucky you." Charles made passage through the doorway. "Lucky me."

We have always felt this man behaved in a manner inappropriate for the father of our husband. Charles Dodds promised fidelity to one woman and broke it with another. Charles Dodds gave his love neither singly nor solely. Charles Dodds allowed his passions to run parallel to an unworthy multitude. We have always felt our husband could have never been the son of such a man. All our worries were for naught.

Despite the low pay of most house servants, Mary Thorne's home held all kinds of finery and frills. A swatch of Persian carpet hung from bent nails above the mantle. A hand-crank Victor collected dust in the corner. A flagon of Georgia moonshine wept condensation on the counter. Charles took two Ball jars from the shelf and poured a stiff round of drinks, the signature peach whirling in the grain alcohol.

"Sweets to the sweet," Charles said, handing Mary Thorne her drink. They were each stung by 180-proof. "Have you been missing me terrible?"

"Hardly gave it notice."

Charles killed what was left in his glass. He breached the

gap between himself and Mary Thorne. She tasted of fruit. Charles lowered his suspenders that were given as an anniversary present and removed her pinafore that was blotchy from the evening meal. He spooled her stockings down to mid-thigh and let his fingers materialize at her undergarment. She felt of silk. At the same moment, as his lips explored the plumage on her neck's nape and as her tongue traced filigrees along his shoulder blade, the silhouette of a man holding a lamp approached Mary Thorne's house from the direction of the Marchetti family's mansion. Charles noticed it first. He said, "Who do there?"

"Who do where?" Mary Thorne followed his gaze to the window. "Oh Lord. It's Frankie."

"Frankie?"

"You've got to get. Right now."

Even before Charles could muster a response, Mary Thorne had returned her intimates to their rightful place and was shoving him towards the window on the far side of the house. Charles raised the window to its full height, climbed through it, and closed the window behind him just in time to see Mary Thorne welcome the arrival of Franklin Marchetti.

Outside was oppressive. It was as hot and dark as pitch. The heels of Charles's boots slowly descended into the muddy bank of the slough, his socks soaking in the black water that come January would turn black ice. He peered through the window. The subsequent episode available by sight but not by sound, Charles would tell his second wife in later years, reminded him of the rarity shows that cost a penny at the Rankin County Fair. We can see it even now. Franklin stumbled slapdash about the shotgun house—so named because a shotgun can be fired from one end to the other without hitting a wall—in the arrogant, resentful manner of a third-son drunkard. He looked under the four-poster canopy bed with a torn mosquito net. He peered behind the oriental dressing screen catawampus to the corner. All the while, Mary Thorne followed him around the room, attempting to assuage whatever had him in arms. She patted his shoulders. She rubbed his elbows. At last, after looking askance into the rafters, after opening all the cabinets, after staring blank at the empty closet, Franklin grew calm. Mary Thorne took his face in her hands and put her wet lips full on his mouth. They held each other. They pressed their foreheads together. They spoke to each other. Mary Thorne did not notice Franklin notice the two drinks on the table. His hands formed a daisy chain around her throat, the petals of his thumbs interlaced with the stems of his fingers. Who knew such strength lay dormant in wrists that could only wear watches built extra-small by a specialty jeweler in St. Louis? The only reaction Franklin gave after what he had done, body of a woman limp on the floor, mark of her nails red on his face, was the dark spot that crept down the leg of his trousers. A puddle rose at his feet, drip by drip.

At the window, Charles fell straight to his knees, shut his eyes, set his jaw, and was overcome with conniption. We do not pity him. His wife was the last thing on his mind, but she should have been the first. Across the county, some twenty miles and four hours away, Julia Dodds put her children to bed and laid wait for her husband. She busied herself with work. On the potbelly stove bought from a corrupt railroad operator boiled an herbal stew, part witch hazel, part alum, part dandelion root, used by midwives to ease the pain of childbirth. Julia beat the substance until it was black as India ink. Everywhere along the floor, most particular beneath the ladder-back chairs of the dinner table, sat a mess of cedar leaves and shagbark. Julia swept hither and yon with a corn broom. She was emptying the cuspidor and checking the chamber pot when she heard someone stomp across the rickety boards of the porch and rap at the pinewood door of her home.

"What you knocking for, Charlie?" There was no answer. "Don't be playing no games with me."

"I'm looking for the missus of the wicker maker." The voice was a man's voice, but it was not Charlie's voice. "Are you the missus of the wicker maker?"

Although she did not know his name at the time, Julia opened the door to the indistinct sight of Noah Johnson. He stepped closer. The skin of his face was as gauzy, brown, and mottled as a used tea bag. His wasted frame hung loose in his clothes. The structure of one of his eyes reminded Julia of ripples from a rock thrown in a stagnant pond. Even with celluloid in his collar and a tilt bowler on his head, basic elements of Southern gentility, this individual had a touch of the simian about his personage. He smelled like a long day.

"Is your husband Charles Dodds?"

"Yes."

"Did he deliver a shipment of furniture to the Tallyho Plantation?"

"Yes."

"Are you the woman they say has a talent for healing folks?"

"Yes."

"Do you consider your husband a faithful man?"

Noah's clodhopper kept Julia from closing the door. At the casual pace of a good neighbor, he removed his hat and walked into the house. He gave his eyetooth a loud suck. He wandered over to the burbling pot, removed the lid, and lowered his nose into the steam. Julia liked to have died. Somehow she managed to say, "What do you want from me?"

"What do I want, Miss Julia?" Noah Johnson undid his top buttons and placed his hat on the table. "I'm here for some medicine. Got me an ache only you can fix."

Julia told him she didn't want her children to hear.

Around midnight Charles decided it was safe for him to leave Mary Thorne's house. Sickle moonlight cut the starless sky. Neap fog clung to the wet ground. Over the past three hours, Charles had sat in mud and stared at nothing as Franklin Marchetti came to his right mind, panicked, paced, prepared, and left the scene of his crime. Charles considered this moment his only chance for escape. There would be no time to say goodbye to the woman who'd been his lover for seven months, three weeks, and two days.

He could remember the exact date of their first encounter because it coincided with Ash Wednesday. The Marchetti family was Catholic—a faith upheld by a small but substantial enclave around Hazlehurst, in much the same way Judaism was around Meridian—but only for the holy days. Every year the family would spend Mardi Gras with their kinfolk in Louisiana, and every year their house would remain empty for at least a fortnight. On the first day of Lent in 1910, Charles Dodds and Mary Thorne had left their sweat marks on every surface of the Marchetti mansion, including the crisp linens of the master bedroom and the yellow wallpaper in the corridors and the checker cloth on the kitchen table.

The memory of their trespass stuck with Charles as he followed the dirt path to his wagon seven months later. The affair had not been his only mistake. Trust us. After a long while spent lost, his boot heels slipping like ice skates on dewy grass, his pant cuffs snagging like fish hooks on scrub brush, Charles finally found his wagon in a meadow of cattails, butterweed, azalea, and goldenrod. The horse team's breath chuffed against the warm night air. Charles initially planned to return home as usual, but instead he decided to leave town for a few days. This tactic would prove lucky. At the same time Charles traveled north to Jackson, where he intended to stay with his cousin over the weekend, Franklin Marchetti explained to the county sheriff not only the circumstances of his invaluable and irreplaceable house servant's death but also to which family the sheriff owed gratitude for his recent election to public office.

"Yes sir, Mr. Marchetti," said the sheriff, whose chatty wife later gave us a thorough account of the conversation. "I'm your man."

"That is music to my ears."

Franklin told the sheriff that Mary Thorne had been having regular relations with a disreputable black man who'd been on the property earlier in the evening, but Franklin chose not to mention his recent dispatch of Noah Johnson to check on the welfare of the disreputable black man's wife. Conclusions were drawn without discussion. The warrant posted countywide for Charles Dodds' arrest did not have to describe him as armed and dangerous, a murderer and a rapist. All of those details were gotten across by the phrase, "Negro at Large."

Over the last hours of night, a vigilance committee, which

consisted of drowsy field hands from nearby plantations, deputies, councilmen, lawyers, and tipsy patrons of the local bucket shop, began a scour of Copiah County. They would never find the culprit. At the encroach of dawn, Charles reached his cousin's place of business, The Dum Dum Inn, a bawdy house located in the northwest section of Jackson. Its proprietor, Jeremiah "Slim Pick" McDonald, patted the fugitive's back. He told Charles, "About time you made time." Always one for family.

Jeremiah did right by the cousin from his mother's side, giving him a soft bedroll, any choice of whore, and three squares daily. Charles declined the whores. Every morning he drank bad coffee with his cousin next to an unlit four o'clock stove, and every evening he drank good whiskey with a regular john prior to an eight o'clock sunset. He lost three pounds in as many days. He grew the patchy rudiments of a beard. One of the Dum Dum's girls, Liza Mae Andrews, saw him on multiple occasions clutch a woman's garter to his damp face. She recognized the lacy item from page sixteen of the Sears Roebuck catalog. Liza Mae incorrectly assumed it belonged to Charles's wife.

On his fifth day from home, Charles received a Western Union telegram sent by Julia. "marchetti paid visit STOP why did you leave without word STOP children miss you STOP me too STOP bank foreclosure on land." It became clear in further messages over the wire that Franklin Marchetti and his brothers had upheld the grudge against Charles Dodds and his family by hiring plug-hat bagmen to harass the household about Charles's location and by asking the Planter's Union Bank to foreclose on the family's outstanding loan. Charles took the serious news in kind. He understood himself to be a gone case, thought on the situation, felt a penitent resolve, and chose to begin another life upcountry. He hitched a ride in a Model AC runabout to Union Station on Central Street and boarded a northbound 2:20 coach on the Tennessee line of the Illinois Central System. He exited the train in Memphis and rented a house on Handwerker Hill. He adopted the name of Spencer. He earned money through carpentry. Within the year he had met a local seamstress named Serena Daniels and would eventually have two healthy children by her.

Only on rare occasions did Mr. C.D. Spencer of Memphis, Tennessee, communicate with Mrs. Julia M. Dodds of Hazlehurst, Mississippi. Their paucity of correspondence has given us a window into the decline of their relationship. All throughout the first four and a half months of their separation, Charles was barely able to send Julia enough money to rent a room at the cheapest hotel in town. Julia did not tell Charles of her illegitimate pregnancy. Charles did not tell Julia of his common-law marriage. All throughout the second four and a half months of their separation, Julia often raised a lethal dose of laudanum to her lips but always succumbed to the impossible compulsion for survival. Charles sent for his children. Julia said goodbye to her children. Only two of them were left when she went into labor.

The year of 1911 was an eventful one. On December 14, Roald Amundsen, key figure in the Heroic Age of Antarctic Exploration, led the first expedition to reach the South Pole. On March 25, the famous fire at the Triangle Shirtwaist Factory killed 146 people. On November 11, the Great Blue Norther of 11/11/11, biggest cold snap in US history, caused record highs in the afternoon and record lows by sunset, frosting flower beds only recently come into bud and bursting pipes in the few houses with waterworks. On March 8, International Women's Day was celebrated for the first time. On October 24, Orville Wright flew through the air for nine minutes and forty-five seconds in a glider at Kill Devil Hills, North Carolina, setting a world record that would stand for a decade. On July 24, Hiram Bingham rediscovered Machu Picchu. On August 22, da Vinci's *Mona Lisa* was stolen from the Louvre. And on May 8, 1911, Robert Johnson was born a bastard.

His name at birth was Robert Leroy Spencer. Despite the conditions of Julia's delivery—teeth marks perforating a leather strop, wooden forceps eddying in pink water—Robert came into this world void of any real physical harm. Covering his face was an amniotic caul, and covering his retina was a mild cataract. The first time his mother held him in her weak arms, however, she focused on the former rather than the latter. Cauls ran in her family. At the time of her recovery, senses intact and mobility firm, Julia let the caul dry until it was a hard sheet and spread it onto a crude block of heartwood and set it in place with silver hobnails. She would eventually take the plaque to her grave in a colored-folk cemetery outside Commerce, Mississippi.

Bessie and Carrie, the two daughters left of Julia's estranged husband, gave their hands to help in raising their youngest brother. They undertook the difficult task, year after year, of masculinizing his childhood. In autumn, they taught him how to sit on cardboard stolen from storerooms and sled down hillsides covered in pine straw. In spring, they let him hold a cane pole, fasten the nightcrawler, and bob for brim at a nearby swimming hole. The main education Robert received from his sisters, all things aside, was how to manipulate the women in his life. What could keep a boy as sharp, as quick, as shrewd from learning the most valuable, the most elusive lesson of manhood?

Shortly after Robert's fifth birthday, Julia and her family of four were evicted from their second home for nonpayment of taxes, due once again to the bureaucratic intervention of the three Marchetti brothers. This time she had no choice in the matter. Julia knew she could not afford to forebear the upbring of her children all on her own. In a letter dated June 24, 1916, found decades later hidden next to a bottle in a rolltop desk at a country yard sale, Julia Dodds wrote to Charles Spencer, "I can no longer make right to raise your two daughters and your son. You have a son. His name is Robert. I do not ask for you to accept me to your home. A labor camp in the Delta, where I can put to use the two things that when idle do the devil's work, will keep me for the season. I ask you to provide for Carrie, who is now eight, Bessie, who is now twelve, and Robert, who is now five. Robert already takes after you." At the end of this letter, one of the most prized in our collection, Julia's signature appears extravagantly wrought, loops round and curves smooth, its dark ink accentuated by what seems the mark of raindrops.

Julia put her children in the back of a tin lizzie on a hot, bright day in the middle of August and saw them for what she thought was the last time through a haze of dust, exhaust, and gnats. Along the way to Memphis, they subsisted on boiled peanuts and pickled peaches from roadside stands, played "Spot the Tree Bear" to pass the time, hummed "Farmer in the Dale" to forget the heat, and waved at the other automobiles that became more diverse every mile farther north. The children reached their destination by noon the next day. They set their ashen knuckles to the door and became a part of the Spencer household one at a time, each met by the man two of them had not seen in almost six years. Robert was last.

The true identity of Robert's father, Charles would claim until he died of a heart attack at age fifty-four, was forever the neighbor of suspicion, doubt, and ignorance. On the day he first opened the door and looked on Robert's bad eye, its lens opaque at center, its lid slouchy in contour, Charles surely must have known Noah Johnson had never been kicked by a mule. A whistle blew soft in the distance. A cloud brought shadow to the lawn. Charles said nothing to the boy, had an itch at his wrist, and let the door allow for entry.

CHAPTER TWO

Over breakfast Leroy Spencer told his younger brother the gift would have to wait 'til after lunch. It was our husband's twelfth birthday. At the kitchen table in the split-level tenement on Handwerker Hill's south side, Robert upheld the appeal to his brother for some kind of hint concerning his birthday present. He asked Leroy, "Is it bigger than a breadbox?"

"Won't tell."

"Animal, vegetable, or mineral?"

"You got the wax in your ears again?" Leroy balled his napkin and lobbed it at his brother. "I said I'm not saying. Don't ask again."

"Is it in this room?"

Since his introduction to the household seven years back, over which time his mother yet seldom sent word, Robert had been so ignored by his father that the only person who gave him any mind was the oldest of his five sisters and six brothers. Leroy was twenty-seven. He worked days as a millwright at the Sperry Lumber Yard in Germantown and nights as a handyman at the Peabody Hotel on Union Avenue. He could clean the breech of a double barrel with a corncob and he could speak two languages of the Five Civilized Tribes and he could whistle any melody after a first listen. He kept in his closet a pinstripe suit cut slim of fine-grade tropical wool. He had a steady girlfriend most of the time, never drank but a drop, never partook of tobacco, and went to the early service on special occasions. Robert idolized him.

"Got some things need getting done," Leroy said from his seat at the gateleg table, sopping his plate with cornbread. "You promise to behave, you get your present."

"Cross my heart. Hope to die."

"I'll be back in a few hours." Leroy walked to the single-bowl scullery sink, lathered his plate, paused at the ledge-and-brace threshold door, settled his hat, and turned the brass knob clockwise by half. "Don't go running all over town while I'm gone."

During those early years of his childhood, Robert Johnson, future guitarist, future singer, future lyricist, had known the world of Memphis to be a world at harmony with itself. Teams of horses would clip-clop their heavy hooves down Cotton Row, pulling wagons teeming with the season's crop. Robert heard them. Merchants would sell their wares, newly improved hand tools and gimcrack beauty products and miraculously curative medicines, with the refrain of "Come and get, folks, come and get." Robert heard them. On Sundays, the scratch choir at First Methodist Church in the Pinch District would sing the gospel by way of psalms, spirituals, and hymns from the Good Book. Robert heard them. On Fridays, the crowds at the local dog track, half a month's pay on the line, would cheer their hardscrabble picks. Robert heard them. On Mondays, the lunch counter at Smith's Rexall Drugs across from the courthouse would brim with tales of famous lawmen dead and promoted to Glory. Robert heard them. The blow of a horn from paddleboats, barges, and flatkeels would echo against the craggy bluffs of the

Mississippi, and the whistle of a steam gong would signal the workday at the city's paper mills, cotton gins, and dairy plants. Robert heard them. The distant susurrus of metal on metal would fill the rich air of Shelby County as Pullman cars stole their way inch by inch across the Harahan Bridge. Robert heard them. In the mornings, he heard thousands of crickets wail their vibrato from the thick leaves of chinaberry clusters. At noon, he heard wind chimes made of bent forks and old knives peal a clarion call from the flower gardens of Elmwood Cemetery. In the evenings, he heard hundreds of locusts scream their falsetto from the brittle branches of sycamore stands. At midnight, he heard the report of Derringers, Colts, and Winchesters burst chaotic from the dark alleys of Beale Street. Everywhere he heard stones in his passway. Everywhere he heard hellhounds on his trail. Everywhere he heard the crossroads at night.

On his twelfth birthday, thanks to the vow of a present, Robert Johnson chose to spend the hot morning hours practicing his chords in the backyard rather than exploring the various neighborhoods of Memphis. His undershirt stuck to his skin and his hands got soggy in the palm as he put the house behind him and strode across the yard. Summer had come early. Although the outdoor thermometer given gratis by the Chero-Cola distributor often reached the vicinity of triple digits—"Cool Yourself Down," it read, "With a Glass of Royal Crown"—the broad canopy of a live oak strung with a Dunlop whitewall provided the backyard generous cover from the noontime sun. Robert laced the long, slender digits of his young hands and waited for a good, loud crack from each knuckle. He knelt at the base of the live oak, bit the inside of his cheek, and went to work on the diddley bow.

Our mutual husband told each of us about the construction of diddley bows during our respective courtships. He said to Mary Sue, "You hammer four or six nails into the trunk of a tree," counting on her fingertips. He said to Betty, "You run some fine wire from one nail to another," with his hands at her hair. He said to Claudette, "You pluck the strings up high near its throat," with his lips at her pulse. He said to Helena, "You slide a glass bottle down it for tonality," lifting her A-line skirt. "It's simple," Robert told each of us at dawn the next day. "Just like love."

Leroy got back home at two in the afternoon. He stood his horse in the gravel thoroughfare, looking down on his younger brother. In one hand he held the fraying reins of the best tack he could afford at his pay, and in the other he carried a cumbersome box wrapped in layers of newsprint. Leroy asked his brother how long he'd been at practice.

"Since you left." Robert dusted his knees and indicated the package. "That my present?"

"Expect so."

Leroy told his brother to wait on the front porch until he'd taken care of his horse in the stall out back. Robert did as told. On about five minutes later, Robert knew his brother was coming close by the sound of him whistling an old ragtime ditty. Leroy appeared from around the corner with the newsprint package in hand. He took the bootworn steps of the porch two at a time, only to heave the present to his tenterhook brother four from the top. Robert thought on its contents for the moment. It could be one of those burlesque magazines, *Photo Bits* or *Body in Art*, he saw on the top shelf at the five-and-dime down the street. It could be the special kind of twill fedora with a paisley ribbon Leroy wore at a tilt when taking girls on the town. Robert hastily tore away the newspaper in sheaths of black and white, the crumpled headlines for May 8, 1923, announcing the recent ceremonial inauguration of Yankee Stadium in New York City and the possible ratification of a law requiring the Ku Klux Klan to publish a list of its members.

His birthday present was a Stella concert guitar. Its brown-finish wooden fingerboard included dot inlays along the frets, its sound hole had a rosette design, and its six-string configuration featured a classic tuner headstock: The instrument was beautiful, luxurious, and ghastly. A guitar meant Robert would actually have to play it; a guitar meant Robert would actually have to be good.

"Where'd you get the money for this?" he asked Leroy, whom we would later question through the bars of his cell at Angola, where he was serving 10-to-20 for bank robbery after a steady eight-year descent into iniquity. "They give you a raise at the lumber yard?"

"I tried my hand at the tables. Beginner's luck."

The first twelve years of Robert Johnson's childhood, regardless of his present concerns, could be seen as a paradigm of musical development. At the age of nine he'd proven himself a quick study of the harmonica and Jew's harp under his brother's patient tutelage. At the age of six he'd glued Coca-Cola poptops to the soles of his saddle shoes and danced taps on the granite slabs in his neighbor's barn lot. At the age of eight he'd taught himself the mechanics of percussion by slapping spoons against the flank of his thigh. What frightened Robert Johnson about owning a guitar, however, was its undeniable, inescapable portent of maturity. Guitars were for men.

"You got to name it," his older brother said through a handsome grin. "Every guitar's got to have a name."

At the same moment Robert was going to tell Leroy he had no such inkling, he heard his own name spoken by someone standing on the sidewalk in front of the house. Robert squinted against the sunlight and wiped sweat from his brow what better to catch sight of a woman leaning against the mailbox stenciled with the counterfeit name of C.D. Spencer. The past years had been hard on her for certain, hair gone gray, cane in hand, face left wrinkly, but she still cut a powerful figure much the same. Robert gripped his guitar and managed to say, "Momma."

Our husband spent the next few years living with his mother in Robinsonville, Mississippi, a sharecropper settlement in the northwest corner of the Delta. During those idylls of his youth—chopping cotton at the Abbay & Leatherman Plantation outside of a town called Commerce, reciting the alphabet at a one-room schoolhouse built along the banks of Indian Creek—Robert Johnson never forgot the strain of his life's ambition. He practiced on "Julia" every chance come his way.

One afternoon when Robert was fourteen, his mother found him playing the Stella six-string in an empty bathtub left for rubbish in a field near their house. The acoustics of cast iron suited the instrument's sound. Robert was busy learning how to use the key of a sardine can as a guitar pick, but he cut his song short when he noticed his mother crossing the field. She sat on the bathtub's roll rim and said, "Fiddle sounds right sweet."

"I guess so."

"I mean it, dear heart."

"I know so."

"Listen here a minute. I'm sorry about what happened this morning. I shouldn't ever do such a thing to you." Julia's eyes followed the trajectory of a bumblebee, but nary a flower blossomed along the ground. "It's just that when you asked me about the thing you did, all grown up and the like, I realized you take after somebody I knew a long time back."

"Take after who?"

"That's why I'm sitting here talking to you now. Got something to tell you. It's about time you were knowing about it. And I didn't want Dusty to hear."

It cannot be said Robert got along with his stepfather. Straw boss of roughly eighty-five tenant sharecroppers around Commerce, respectable deacon in a local congregation, and modest resident of Tunica County for all of fifty-one years, William "Dusty" Willis was given his nickname because he had a tendency to walk so fast a cloud of dust would billow around his feet and legs. He did not allow for spare moments. Dusty Willis thought of his second wife's son as a spoilt city boy whose guitar was the devil's tool. He called it a pitchfork.

"Dusty doesn't want to hear nothing, Momma."

"Anything."

"Dusty doesn't want to hear anything, Momma."

"He's done his best to raise you like you were his own son. Past couple years he's kept food over your head and a roof on the table. But Dusty's not your father. You never even met him."

"How's that now?"

"The father you know isn't your real father." Julia swept a cow killer from her threadbare knee-high, frowning at the bug's coat of red and black fuzz. "You're not a Spencer. You're not a Dodds. You know you're not a Willis. Your real father's name was Johnson."

Julia told her son about a "love affair" she had with "the kindest, gentlest man" around the time of her husband's departure for Memphis. She told him how her husband, try as he might, never forgave the sin. She told him of her own guilt over the "union at night" whose only consequence worth mention was the "blessing of his birth." At the end of his mother's confession, Robert said not a word to her—he had questions plenty, but answers would come—even as she stood from the tub broken beyond repair, even as she left the grassy field scattershot with clover.

What stuck longest with Robert was the name of Johnson. During the years to follow, he felt it necessary to adopt the name as his own, but he couldn't bring himself to tell anyone the truth. To Ms. Pamela Lafayette, headmistress of the Indian Creek School, he remained Little Bobby Spencer, the boy with poor eyesight and beautiful script who sat in the third row from the back. To Mr. Samuel Oglethorpe, overseer of the Abbay & Leatherman Plantation, he remained Dusty Willis Junior, a farmhand earning a dollar a day to wield a hoe through clumps of buck brush. Robert Johnson never told anyone his real name until the day he met our predecessor.

On Saturday, April 11, 1928, Robert Johnson decided he would run away from home. Such thoughts were nothing new. Earlier in the evening, just as usual, Robert's stepfather had forbidden him to attend the Saturday night ball held regular in a barn behind the Robinsonville Mercantile, and later in the evening, just as usual, Robert put a row of feather pillows beneath his patchwork coverlet and snuck out his bedroom's double-hung sash window. He had yet to get caught.

The Robinsonville Mercantile was a good hour away, but Robert made it there in forty-five minutes easy. Tonight was special. Son House and his crew, legends throughout the dance halls of the Delta, bluesmen of bluesmen, professionals along the circuits of the South, were expected to arrive from a gig in Fayetteville and begin their first set at nine o'clock. Although most Saturday night balls didn't get up running 'til well past ten, "The Godfather of Blues Music" could draw an early crowd by virtue of reputation alone. Somewhere close to a hundred souls were milling about the dry goods stock when Robert arrived at the scene his stepfather would often refer to as the devil's larder.

He joined a group of friends from the county, Johnny Boyd Johnson, Frank Diamond, Harpo Wells, Curtis Peters, Albert Tad Lipscomb, and Johnny Shines, who over the next nine years would accompany Robert to St. Louis, Charleston, Toronto, and New York. All of them were talking biggity about their talents in relation to Son House—"I can play circles around him" and "He got nothing hear-tell over me"—when the man himself walked through the crowd past them towards the barn. Afterwards, the boys scarce made a sound except until a girl standing near them did.

"Catmightydignifiedtilthedogwalkby."

At first Robert thought she was speaking in the unknown tongue. Even though her words were intelligible, they reminded him, with their muddled vowels, with their blurred consonants, of the box suppers, protracted meetings, and tent revivals that had grown popular throughout the better part of the region. Robert observed the girl. She wore a blue-and-white gingham dress, soft furbelow grazing her kneecaps. The curvatures at her elbows, neckline, and ankles were as naked as the day Jesus flung them. She bore the evidence of store-bought soap, hints of sassafras oil, mint, lemon, salt, and vegetable tallow. At her side she held by suction of her thumb a Coca-Cola, its hobbleskirt bottle filled just partly with the original mix. Her breath suggested bourbon.

"My name's Robert Johnson." He came the closer. "What's your name?"

"Virginia Travis."

What he didn't know at the time but would soon learn through conversation was that she had been born under a harvest moon sixteen and a half years earlier, her golden retriever's name was Maybeetle Purslane Socrates, her father owned forty acres of good bottomland, her favorite flavor of ice cream was spumoni, and a childhood case of the mumps had taken her ability to hear.

"How can you tell what I'm talking at you right now?" Robert gave her a second. "How…can…you tell…what I'm…talking…at…you right now?"

"The same way I know what's in a book," Virginia said with laughter. She placed her index finger on the philtrum of his lip. "I know how to read, thunk you headly."

Those last words sunk it for him. While ignoring the cat calls and dog barks from his friends, some apparently jealous of this girl's beauty, others outright disdainful of this girl's handicap, Robert slipped Virginia's hand into his jittery own, walked through the lessening crowds, and entered the barn in time to witness Son House take a seat on a three-leg stool and strike the very first licks of the night. It wasn't the only traveling band Robert had ever seen, but it certainly was a sight he'd ever laid eyes. At lead guitar, Son House, who years earlier had been a Baptist minister and who a year later would shoot a Texan allegedly in self-defense, channeled hellfire into his performance, hands nothing but a confusion of strum, sweat raining down on the fingerboard, eyes anything but steady in their aim, and voice railing against the authority from on high. At second guitar, Willie Brown, who would be the only person Robert Johnson said should get notified in the event of his death and who remains forever the "my friend-boy" referenced in the lyrics of "Cross Road Blues," could hardly keep up to comment, his hands stumbling across the strings, his face contorted into concentration. The crowd sure did hully-gully on the dirt floor. They swung their arms like the tarnashun and they threw their legs like a hootenanny. One story has it that a baby fell out of its mother's womb during a dance called Cloud Nine, the umbilical cord left to shrivel away on the ground's layer of dust, manure, and straw. Another story has it that a steamboat deckhand bled from his ears without even a touch of soreness, the red stain on his collar so elaborately patterned that people thought he'd been given one of the Five Sacred Wounds.

"Why would you come to these things," Robert said to Virginia, "if'ing you can't hear what they play?"

Virginia stared at one of the barn's supportive beams. She took Robert's hand and placed it on the wood. The music's vibrations shimmied through his fingertips. She pointed at the ground, stomped her foot, and nodded at the crowd. The dance's rhythms bound up his leg. Robert shook the more at the memory of her touch.

With a smirk Virginia said she wanted to dance and left him on his own with a fresh erection. The barn was hotter than all get-out. At close to 102.4 degrees, the air could not be distinguished from the people in it, and at close to 98.6 degrees, the people could not be distinguished from the air around them. Robert lost Virginia. Her invention of style should have set her apart, but he could not tell anything from the mass of bodies in motion.

All that survives of Virginia since she went to her reward is a sepia-tone cameo found in a drab pewter locket. The very features that stand out in the small photograph, the delicate coincidence of her fingers and hair, a tiny pearl of sweat at her temple, the russet brown coordinating her skin and eyes, allowed Robert to find her in the crowd at the Saturday night ball. The flower vine of his pulse, as he put his hands at her lower back, as he set his feet in accord with her own, scaled the latticework of his desire. They danced in the company of others. They danced in the company of others. They danced in the company of others. The realization of what Robert was feeling did not occur to him against the twelve-bar arrangement so essential to the origins of blues music, nor did it occur on the 3-4-3 beat he would eventually master in his own songs. He fell in love between sets.

Outside, where they sought the cool of midnight air, Robert pulled a harmonica from his pocket, cradled it in his palms, and serenaded Virginia with sound. She held her hand against his chest so she could register the notes of music. At the end of the song, she leaned towards his ear and whispered, "Be the fool."

"What?"

"Beautiful."

The marriage ceremony of Robert Johnson and Virginia Travis would be held at the Commerce Missionary Baptist Church on Sunday, January 21, 1929.

What little we know of Robert and Virginia's life together was drawn piecemeal from our husband at those rare times of his capitulation to sorrow, remembrance, and whiskey. Their marriage took a beat all its own. Although chores on the homeplace kept them apart throughout the day—her churning cow milk into sweet butter, him thatching raw burlap to burst pipes—Robert and Virginia spent their nights sitting with their hands at common prayer before the commencement of a meal, strolling the countryside in step to the songbirds of sundown, and whispering persiflage ear to ear in the candlelit hours after retirement to bed. Soon enough, one thing leading to another, another leading to one thing, our predecessor found herself in a family way.

They'd been wed ten months when Virginia went into labor. On his arrival home from work at the Abbay & Leatherman, where he still got paid a meager wage for tending the scraggly cotton fields and where he still got lost in his head arranging clumsy song lyrics, Robert opened the door of his home, sump mud stuck to his boots, guitar slung across his back, to find his wife sitting in a puddle of liquid on the floor. Her fingers were splayed across her belly. Her breath came and went on the quick. Her eyes were glazed to the light. Robert fell to his knees, took his wife's hand, and said, "Is it time?"

She did not answer out loud. Virginia let her uncertain gaze travel from her husband's face wrung into confusion, across her dress spotty at the waist, across her hands shaking beyond control, to the puddle on the floor marbling with far too much blood. In it she had written with her finger a single six-letter word.

Within the hour Robert had reached the doctor's office by foot and ridden with him back to the house. Dr. Netherland brought a midwife for assistance. At the sight of Virginia on the floor, agonized, bloody, petrified, both the doctor and his midwife, the former arranging steel instruments and lifting the patient's wet skirt, the latter fetching a white-cooper's bucket of spring water, filling a stockpot on the sheet-iron stove, and stoking the firebox until the water hit a boil, reacted in a manner unlikely, inhuman, and unearthly in comparison to Robert Johnson, whose limbs went rigid and whose face went slack, his only audible reaction the subterranean moan of a young man come to his first absolute grief.

"You have to be staying outside," the doctor told him. "I can't be having you in here."

"Why?"

"Boy."

"Okay."

"Miss Burchill, bring me the chloroform pills," the doctor told her. "Help me get this woman on the bed and out of this muck."

On the porch, Robert got a tenuous handle of his constitution, trying not to listen. A barn owl took silent flight from its perch in a lone cedar and sank its talons into some opossum whose shriek broke the sylvan calm. Junkyard dogs on a nearby farm howled and barked and growled against the darkness of cotton fields at night. A pair of whitetail fawn stood at a salt lick until the rustling of a copperhead near their feet set them to gallop in tandem far from earshot. Around the other side of midnight, some two and a half hours later, Dr. Netherland opened the door and waited for Robert's company.

"Your wife had some complications made a struggle of the birth." The two men regarded each other. "I have some news may be hard to hear."

"I know."

"The child."

"I know."

"The mother."

"I know."

"Even if we'd gotten here before it begun, I don't know as it could've gone about otherwise." The two men looked away from each other. "Had you and the missus given your child a name? I need it for the certificate."

Our husband kept so quiet. At plain sight of the doctor and his midwife, one removing his sleeve garters in dire need of a wash, the other spreading muslin cloth atop a willow basket, Robert stumbled down the front porch's creaky steps wrought slantwise with lost-head nails, caught his breath, walked among crickets whose chirping foretold the approach of dawn, hung his head, and stopped in tall grass overrun with nut sedge, foxtail, and coffee weed. He held himself against the cold. He sank his gaze to a low spot. Whatever his thoughts were throughout the night—we do not know for certain if he cursed God, but we do know he had ample provocation—Robert Johnson's son remains nameless to this day.

⁂

He knew it was the end, but he could not end it. At Scotty Jay's Rumpus Room near Baton Rouge, Louisiana, one of the roughest honk-a-tonks within legal distance of the parish limits, a whorehouse with no whores, a pool hall with no pool, where men came to drink and gamble but nothing much else except be men, Robert Johnson was dealt a string of hands that put him $157 in the hole. All that was left to whatever name he was going by at the time sat on the worn felt of an old card table in the dark parlor. Two white chips at twenty-five cents apiece, one red chip worth five dollars, two blue chips at a dollar each. Anybody of sound reason would have called it a night.

"Praise the Lord almighty above if Robert isn't my new favorite player," said Ferris Thurgood, cardsharp and hothead, who'd once cut a priest's vestigial tab clean in half for fobbing his excess chips in the manner a cheat would some stray ace. He said, "Feel free to sit your raggedy ass across from me anytime you want."

"Ain't that wit."

"I can't feature why Robert here always got that guitar with him," said Woodson Potter, yards of rye in his gut, sideiron on the table, plug of chaw in his lip, whose minacious smile drew attention from a face ugly with pox scars. He said, "Hasn't played a lick since I known him. Must be his lucky charm."

"Just you wait."

The evening's game was five-card stud. Although he would eventually curtail the progress of such a low habit, Robert could never fully quit his compulsion. We know from experience. Around about the time of their introduction, he taught Claudette a standard game variation, "Follow the Queen," whereby every card dealt face-up following a queen becomes wild until the appearance of another queen. During their courtship, he gave Tabitha lessons in community card play. During their engagement, he gave Betty lessons in cards-speak split pot. Around about the time of their marriage, he told Mary Sue how the king of hearts is often known as a suicide king and how the queen of spades is often known as a bedpost queen. We never gave it much mind.

On the night at the bar, still a few years from his proposal to the first of us, Robert Johnson, strung on all sides by railbirds anonymous in their numbers, played Ferris Thurgood and Woodson Potter in a type of five-card stud called "Dr. Pepper Poker." The popular soft drink's slogan, "Drink a bite to eat at 10, 2, and 4 o'clock," inspired the special variant in which the ten, two, and four cards were wild.

Each of the players placed their ante of fifty cents at the center of the tabletop. Woodson was on the button. First he dealt a card face-down, and next he dealt a card face-up. At sight of his ace of clubs and eight of spades, Robert tossed five dollars worth of chips into the pot, a goodly portion of his final stake, and at third and fourth street's advent of a queen of diamonds and an ace of spades, he raised the pot by another fifty cents in chips, leaving him with only two dollars. The others called him each round. Robert felt there must be a cinch hand somewhere in his draw, but the deck would not oblige him beyond the nut. His next card, lest he come a cropper, surely had it. Thus, on fifth street, his pulse slowing near to a crawl, his palms going dry as goofer dust, Robert was dealt an eight of clubs to complete his two-pair hand of dark suits.

"Look at him now, I tell it, look at him now," either Ferris or Woodson said as both of them raised the pot higher than their opponent's last two dollars. "Robert got the *malaise*. He got the malaise like he never been to Louisiana."

He'd been to Louisiana all right. Since our predecessor's death less than two years back, Robert Johnson had passed transient throughout the counties and states and townships of the South, never once arriving without the same intention in mind, never once leaving without failure to achieve it. Much can be told of a man by the way he goes about killing himself. Robert stole at the glint of his knife every kind of transportation along the Natchez Trace, steam railcars to phaetons to horseless carriages, each vehicle's Klaxon bell scaling the pitch of his mad laughter. He was known then as Carter. Robert committed acts of congress with a host of slatterns from Storyville, mulattoes and high browns and darkies, only some of whose standards of hygiene involved the protection of a pessary. He was known then as Jones. Robert kissed the dainty hand of a plantation owner's beautiful daughter outside of a Woolworth's Store and provoked a lynch mob into searching every alley of Frontage Street for "the sambo who raped a debutante," only to escape their howls for mortal retribution by putting on white face along with a black hat and kvetching Yiddish polyglot in mimicry of a minstrel show remembered from his Memphis childhood. He was known then as Goldstein. Robert was arrested once in Georgia for expectoration on a public sidewalk and was found guilty three times in Alabama for collusion to vagrancy and was sentenced twice in Florida for public intoxication. He was known then as Smith. Robert Meriwether commandeered an Oldsmobile Curved Dash over the side of a suspension bridge straight into the shallow chop of the Black Warrior River. Robert Simpson stood in a pasture of Yalobusha County during a thunderstorm with a steel railway sleeper raised high above his head. Robert Boswell stenciled zigzag scars on his thin wrists with a Sheffield straight razor pinched from J.P. Nettle's Shaving Shop on Fat Tuesday. All the same, despite the many signs of providence—his unconscious body burping from the brown waters due to buoyancy from a geological salt inclusion, lightning bolts melting rivets on a distant barn's tin roof, his blade cutting but scratches because its previous owner was a barber compulsively frugal with his tools—our husband considered his own survival to be nothing more and nothing less than the hardest, worst, dumbest luck.

"How far will this get me?" Robert put his guitar in the pot. "I'm feeling fortunate this evening."

Between piles of chips worth about thirty dollars, the Stella concert guitar, later sold at Sotheby's for $8,450 not including tax, sat at the center of the table, kerosene light reflected in its varnish, cheroot smoke wafting over its strings. Ferris and Woodson exchanged a look of confusion on the mend. At the moment one of them was about to speak, a voice from the back of the crowd said, "It's a damn sight for a bluesman to gamble his guitar."

Robert couldn't believe it from make-believe. That voice cured by cheap whiskey, those wrists stained in black powder. This man could not be his brother. The dim bar did not allow for easy sight, but this man could not possibly be his brother. Robert told him as much.

"I should say the same," said Leroy, only two months,

three weeks, and five days from his induction to the country's worst hoosegow, where decades later he would join a group of inmates, "Angola's Heel Street Gang," who cut their own Achilles' tendons in protest of the poor conditions. "I think we're both about close to bottom."

"What're you—"

Robert's words were cut short by the realization he had accidentally laid all of his cards face-up on the table. Woodson and Ferris in turn laid down their own cards, two at a time and then one at a time, the former holding a straight flush with queens high, the latter holding a full house of jacks over nines. The demure smiles on each face card seemed a weird simulacrum of each man's devious grin. It suddenly became apparent that Robert Johnson, who would later win two Grammy's within sixteen years, who would later be among the first thirteen musicians inducted into the Rock and Roll Hall of Fame, who would later go multi-platinum three times with only twenty-nine songs, had lost his guitar in a single hand of poker.

Our husband could not find the words, let alone the actions, though his opponents had no such problem. Woodson gave his winnings a home at his side as Ferris put on a spectacular show of flatulence. Finally, after he knocked over his chair while standing up, after he mumbled some such nonesuch to his brother's offer of help, after he dribbled sweat on the table while backing away, Robert made to take leave of Scotty Jay's Rumpus Room. The upstairs girls marked the cross from shoulders to forehead. The knuckledusters searched their cups for a sign of divination. On the porch, leaning over the scrapwood rail and aiming for a dandelion patch, Robert evacuated the contents of his stomach, including five pints of the house lager, three quail eggs, the lobe of a pig's ear pickled in pink vinegar, a dozen cove oysters, the oily shreds of tobacco loosed from a cheap cigarette, and seven wheat-head pennies he always swallowed before a night of gambling. He retrieved his last seven cents by hand.

The gorgeous, bold, painful sunlight of the early morning hour affected Robert much as like an insult were tipping its hat to an injury. He'd thought the day had only just come round to night. Where was his moon? Where were his stars?

On arrival outside, Leroy gave his brother a handkerchief, telling him to wipe the yuck from around his mouth. Robert accepted the offer, did as he was told, and returned the hankie, at which point Leroy bloodied his brother's lips with the stern version of a hand.

"Look at yourself. Take a step back and look at yourself." The Adam's apple bobbed in Leroy's throat. "You're filthy. You're drunk. I ought to slap you *twice* upside the head."

"I lost my one only wife!"

"You're a disgrace. I'm ashamed to call you my brother. Flat broke, degenerate, no-account, gambling badman."

"She was my one only love!"

"What would Momma think of you now?" Leroy's voice collapsed to a whisper. "What would Momma say to you right this instant? May her sweet soul rest in peace."

"Momma's dead?"

It was at that very moment, our husband of so few years would tell each of us, he felt the strangest comfort in his heart. How still he must have stood. How quiet he must have kept. On such a beautiful day, magnolia blossoms shimmering with beads of dew, mockingbirds whistling songs to the dawn, he found the clarity that only comes after the realization that grief in this world will never end. The decision all but made itself. Robert Johnson shook his oldest brother's hand for the first time with a man's grip, brushed the dust from his weskit, placed a derby cap under his arm, and took easy but wary flight along a tar-bound macadam highway, his eventual destination the place just beyond where one road meets another.

PART TWO

"Traveling Riverside Blues"

On his birthday in the early summer of 1995—*The Blues Almanack* incorrectly claims May 5, just three days shy of right—we began visiting our mutual husband's assortment of graves. The six of us took pilgrimage from our homes in cities such as Dallas, Montreal, and New York, from our families that span three generations and seven decades, from our lives spent votive to the memory of our paramour of the twelve-bar, our Lazarus of the six-string. The maps of Mississippi thumbtacked to our walls indicate with red flags the eight possible gravesites of Robert Johnson. We visited each and every one.

At the time, we all knew of our collective existence, but none of us had ever met the other. Perhaps if this were not the case, our lives would have taken paths less divergent. Perhaps if we had known each other, we would not be such an eclectic group. Three of us graduated from college, one summa cum laude, another magna. Two of us are left-handed. One of us is half white. Five of us can knot cherry stems with our tongues, and three of us can whistle after eating Saltines. Two of us shook the hands of presidential first ladies. Three of us survived the big ones of '52, '71, and '89, two of us met the Chicago seven, six of us adore the Jackson Five, and four of us caught foul balls in the ninth inning of game six. One of us is rich, one of us is famous, one of us is both. Two of us are indexed in encyclopedias and search engines, each of whom can be cross-referenced via the subjects "Choice, pro" and "Rights, civil." Some of us distress film audiences with our tears during low comedies and our laughter during high dramas. Most of us love our children as much as our children's children. All of us exceeded, whether acknowledged or not, the bounds and expectations placed on our race, class, and gender by society and country, by humanity and the world, by ourselves and each other. In truth and in short, we are all extraordinary individuals. Such was why it seemed that, rather than circumstance or coincidence, the mysterious yet fathomable hands of fate compelled each of us, all unbeknownst to the other, to visit the eight possible gravesites of our husband, Robert Johnson, in the last decade of the century in which he lived his paltry twenty-seven years.

Mary Sue first felt the quasi-religious draw to his burial ground. In May of 1995, she returned to Mississippi from her three-story brownstone on New York's Upper East Side. She drove a rented Mercedes in the discomfort of stilettos and scorn. She looked at the impoverished state of her birth through the lenses of sunglasses and a fifty-year absence. At the third supposed gravesite of our former husband, which she reached near dusk on her first day, Mary Sue finally decided she'd found the last home of Robert Johnson, as she could feel his presence, his spirit hovering like black noise all around her. The lichen-mottled gravestone, a lowercase "x" its only clue to the identity of the body two yards below, jutted from soybean stubble in a field outside of Friars Point, Mississippi. Mary Sue's heels sank in the river-moistened soil. Her hands fumbled with a lighter and cigarette. At that moment, as she exhaled a sweet stream of smoke and as her skin turned gooseflesh with bale, an otherworldly quiet overtook the deltic flatness. At that moment, too, Mary Sue knew for certain she stood in the presence of Robert Johnson's ghost. She knew that he was at peace and that he was asking for her forgiveness.

Betty, who searched for his true burial place a year later, did not encounter our husband's celestial manifestation until the fifth grave she visited. This one was unmarked. According to reliable legend, it lay in a pecan grove just north of Belzoni, and according to less reliable rumor, its exact location was four paces south of the one tree that never produced nut. Betty drove to the spot at night in a two-cylinder jalopy, her motor skills touched by three pints of rotgut. Once there, she stumbled over the ground covered in cedar boughs and their shed bark, pecan shells and their fruit's carrion, oak leaves and their skeletal twigs. The hardwood trees of Mississippi, far more prevalent in the Delta due to its sandy loam soil, are said to be haunted by the slaves of the state's persistent, tragic history. The lyrical creaking of their branches and limbs, so goes the story, eulogizes the pain of the slaves' lives, personifies the release of their deaths, and imports the boon of their transcendence. On that night in a thicket of cedar and pecan and oak, Betty heard not the wails of our ancestors but the warbling of our late husband. His song did not beg clemency or pity. It accused her of betrayal.

Betty had wasted her life on drink, sang Robert Johnson's voice, drowned her soul in the glow of moonshine. She had failed not only him but also herself. As the wind went slack and the song of hardwoods mute, Betty heard footfall throughout the grove, its source cloaked in Mississippi pitch. Someone was out there. Someone was watching her. Betty might have discovered the identity of the trespasser—be it astral bluesman, curious deer, or wayward vagrant—if only her brain did not choose that moment to succumb to the whiskey's somnolent influence. She passed out on a bed of the South's heritage, its silent foliage caressing her into sleep.

Claudette was the last of us to seek our husband's resting place. Although eight possible burial venues existed throughout Mississippi, Claudette knew from her extensive archives that the authentic gravesite probably lay somewhere near Greenwood. There were three likely locations. Robert Johnson's body was most commonly thought to be buried at Mount Zion Missionary Baptist Church, as his death certificate stated he was laid to rest in "Zion yonder." Claudette visited our husband's monument, originally commissioned by Columbia Records, in the dead end of the church's garden, but its lifeless stone obelisk, mildewed list of song titles, and shoddy craftsmanship left her cold. The second possible location was Little Zion Church, just under two miles from the house where Robert Johnson died. Despite the strong evidence in its favor, Claudette knew in her gut and in her heart, be there a difference, that Little Zion, surrounded by pivot irrigation, power towers, land levelers, and grain elevators, was not our husband's final, peaceful place of rest. Only one possibility remained.

The tiny one-stoplight of Quito, Mississippi, home to the Payne Chapel Church, stands just a few miles southwest of Morgan City and Itta Bena. Claudette arrived at the church, built near Mosquito Lake, the town's namesake, around the half-lit hours of dawn. In the graveyard, she found a small marker with Robert Johnson's name underscored by the words,

RESTING IN THE BLUES. On the stone lay several piles of loose change, as though our husband's phantom played eternally next to the grave, his hat upturned at the foot of marble, waiting for payment. Claudette, thinking she was alone in the cemetery, felt certain this was Robert Johnson's actual grave. She may have been right in feeling it was his grave, but she was wrong in thinking she was alone.

Next to the church stood a figure silhouetted by the rising sun. Although she could discern very few details, Claudette somehow knew the figure was the specter of our husband, the ghost of Robert Johnson. That pose favoring his left leg, that balsamic skin with its milky translucence, that wide-brim hat cocked at a rakish tilt, all of it reminded her of the man she had not seen in over half a century. Claudette, our archivist to the very end, reached quickly for the camera in her bag, but when she pulled focus, the apparition had disappeared into the horizon. So Claudette photographed the rising sun, drove home to Dallas, located Quito on her map of Mississippi, and placed a black flag next to the red one. Black represents locations in which we have undeniably felt our husband's spirit.

But how undeniable, we soon asked ourselves, were the encounters? Was that really Robert Johnson's ghost in the disquiet air, among the tree limbs, at the church cemetery? In those strange times, each of us unknown to the other, we did not yet understand the truth. Years later we discovered that what we experienced at our husband's graves, that the ghost of Robert Johnson we felt and heard and saw, sprang figuratively and literally from ourselves. We were his spirit incarnate. We were our own deception. At the gravestone outside Friars Point, Mary Sue did not actually feel the ethereal presence of our husband drifting around her. She felt the presence of the rest of us. At the unmarked grave in the pecan grove, Betty did not actually hear the song of our husband whispering in the hardwoods, the sound of his feet walking through the thicket. She heard the hummed melody and the quiet footsteps of another of us who happened to visit his grave at the very same time. At the tombstone in the cemetery near Quito, Claudette did not see the apparition of our husband standing near the church. She saw another one of us visiting his grave, veiled in billowy black dress, gladiolas and pennies in hand, ready to pay tribute to the man we all had finally come to believe was dead. It was his birthday. Our husband, who was born on May 8, 1911, and who died on August 13, 1938, would have been eighty-four years old.

CHAPTER THREE

Years later, two weeks prior to his death, Robert Johnson would remember Calletta Craft's words as plainly as the chords of a song, but at the moment, ten minutes past midnight on December 12, 1931, he might as well have had cotton pits stuck deep in his ear sockets. "You can play it on the one," Callie said from the player piano across the lobby, "you can play it on the other."

At the Emerald Slipper, a proprietary concern Callie inherited from her first husband, Sargent Craft, after he fell into a nest of water moccasins, Robert was playing on both his harmonica and his guitar, studying how to mimic one's sound on the other. It was a slow night. The nearby town of Martinsville, nothing more than a coalition of pine lumberyards and railway backtracks in the southern part of Mississippi, provided a meager clientele. Although ostensibly a dosshouse for people of a stamp, your sneak thieves, your gandy dancers, your street buskers, the Emerald Slipper got most of its revenue from the cottage industry of flesh. Our husband, who was neither customer nor employee but who had lived there the past four months, took well to being kept.

"Why don't you put that thing down, lover?" Callie straddled the piano bench as a child would a rocking horse. "Why don't you come over and stay awhile?"

"In a second," Robert said. "Just a second."

Callie Craft was a contradiction. She would slap a trickle of blood from the quivering lips of her girls upstairs only to spend hours at night wrapping towels soaked in buttermilk around their lady parts. She would earn money to purchase unnecessary comforts like glad rags from Montgomery Ward by sewing quilts for white women whose Parisian styles she sought for her own closet. The mysterious names of her patchwork designs—Distant Star of Sweet Bedlam, Hobson's Choice, Forbidden Fruit, Lincoln's Platform, Long Road to River Styx—were common parlance among good society. Seven years shy of her fiftieth birthday, widow twice over, and mother of three full-grown children, Callie advocated the belief that everyone's past was best forgotten. She kept a nation sack full of dead scorpions tied around each garter to ward away the spirits of her neverborn.

Robert was busy mumbling to himself, "I said got damn, I said got damn," straining his eyes on the strings, tapping his foot to a rhythm, and experimenting with new finger positions when Callie slinked her way across the bear-pelt rug ornamenting the lobby floorboards, raised his neck hairs from behind with the damp of her breath, slipped her hand over his shoulder towards the trouser crutch, and began torturing his limp prick through the buffer of shoddy gabardine wool. She said, "I need to buy you some new pants. These just will not do."

"If that's what you'd rather," Robert said as he went stiff in her grip, a sunflower to its namesake, "I'm not stopping you."

His glass of white whiskey, still half full after its pour an hour ago, made a sweat ring on the mahogany bar. The tang of creosote throughout the lobby, a result of the Avondale stove beginning to scorch the purple flocked-velvet wallpaper, stood to overwhelm the smell of perfume, hair tonic, and monthlies drifting from the bedrooms overhead. His brogans with their wooden soles, bought on a charge ticket at the county grab-all, rang a coarse noise against the ground. Robert was near to panic when he finally spent himself in those old pants.

Given such distractions, bless his soul, our husband could only practice after a fashion. He needed the consideration we would soon provide him. Callie did not exhibit hardly the prudence of Mary Sue, who every day went for a walk between the hours of three and six. Callie lacked the tender, honest devotion of Betty, who regularly emptied his whiskey bottles in the woodshed. Callie did not possess half the foresight of Claudette, who often gave her children rock candy to keep them quiet. What made her think she could possibly become a better half? How could she ever regard herself as one of the fairer sex? These days we have come to learn that women are always more sensible, except of course whenever the issue happens to concern their sensibilities.

"Let's you and me head up to the bedroom," Callie said. "Momma wants her some milk and honey. Might even let you have some, too."

"I have told you I need to practice for at least another hour."

The lobby was not loud for a little bit.

"I am none too pleased with the tone I'm hearing right now."

"Wish I could say I gave a horse apple in hay," Robert said. "Leave me alone 'til I finish playing this thing. Give me some hush-now so as I can think."

The dowager's gall should warrant its own categorical

distinction amongst the bodily humors. On such harsh words from Robert, Callie Craft carelessly walked towards the bar and carefully wiped her arm across the countertop, sending a dozen glasses crashing to shards on the ground and waking every girl upstairs with the frightful racket. Afterwards, she exited the Emerald Slipper through the saloon doors in front, perhaps to stand on the porch until someone saw fit to attend on her, perhaps to visit the outhouse until the winter chill sent her back inside for warmth. Robert did not once give his eyes to anything other than the guitar.

He was working on a knife piece. Although his face would often appear misleadingly boyish, as each of us failed to realize during those years but as each of us have come to understand so many decades later, Robert Johnson tended to show his true age when he concentrated on music. We can picture him now. The skin about his bad eye may have bunched together like a river in oxbow as he studied on how exactly to place his hand against the fingerboard. His lips may have shrunk to a pucker around the stub of an unlit easy-roll. The hollows of each cheek may have fallen deeper into his overbite of the jaw. His brow may have imitated the rows of a cotton field in tilling season as he cantered the cheap guitar on his thigh and plucked each string with a copper pick. At the Emerald Slipper, Robert was so focused on his music he must not have heard someone enter the lobby behind him—that stomp of boots on the doorsill, an awkward cough, that wallop of a hat losing its crest—nor must he have heard the stranger stop and listen to him play the blues.

"You're doing it all wrong."

On the other side of the room stood a tall, elegant, meticulous, thin man in an ebony frock coat, his Wellingtons dripping grassy midnight dew, his Tyrolean hanging on a coat tree in the corner. Dust came off him like wet from a dog. His skin could not have been darker if it'd been smeared with burnt cork, but his eyes could've only been brighter if they had been wiped in cold cream. He wore on his upper lip the ghost of a pencil moustache. At Robert's attention, the man crossed the room, offering his hand for a shake and saying, "But take heart, young man. I could teach you how to play the guitar. Like you would never dream 'til the coming of rapture."

The man's hand was slippery in the palm, missing a digit, and hot as the flames of hell.

Reverend Ike Zinnerman of Pass Christian, Mississippi, lost his pinkie finger on Black Thursday of the Great Wall Street Crash. Prior to the historic day, he'd been a purveyor of toothpaste, a metallurgist, a veteran of the war with a limp taken in the trenches, a lost relative, a found relative, a victim of highway robbery, an inventor of the perpetual motion device, and a skillful raconteur whose tales of the El Camino Real, Babe Ruth, regal ancestry, the Maginot Line, Dr. Du Bois, x-ray machines, the World's Fair, and petroleum strikes along the Bering Strait never failed to gain him respect, generosity, and zeal from any and all listeners. Reverend Ike may not have been a reverend, but the label honestly did suit his occupation. He ordained the sacraments, preached the gospel, and ministered to worship of the almighty dollar.

On Thursday, October 24, 1929, Reverend Ike was putting on an "Authentic Revival of Campbellite Temperament" near the swampy canebrakes due west of our state capitol. His sermon was known countywide as evangelism in the raw. At a quarter 'til sunset, Reverend Ike took the platform built of yellow pine and stood before a congregation of poor, black laborers. He did not say a word for good on two minutes. Rather than grow restless with such quiet, the members of the crowd, not exchanging their recipes for buttermilk pie, not upsetting ant beds with a stick, not considering painful ingrowths of the nail, became more and more deferential to the figure so struck with piety he could not utter a word. They drew a collective gasp when Reverend Ike said, "Come forward, my flock."

He told them he was a shepherd whose mission was to guide them through the valley of the shadow of death. He told them they would not only weather the storm of persecution like the Israelites lost in the desert for so many years, eating "mantra" fallen from the sky, carrying the ark of the "cabinet," but they would also prevail themselves unto the holy land as the one and only people chosen to receive the Lord's divine glory. He told them he knew the names of their heartbeats. He told them he heard their thoughts as a melody. He told them he understood The Sound of God.

"It is the sound of your heartbeats and your thoughts. It is the sound of salvation, of grace, of paradise, of hope. Have you heard God? It is said that once He enters your soul, at that very instant, music will fill your ears. Pray with me."

Of course, at that very instant, music filled their ears, taking the form of a high-pitched noise with no discernable origin. Dulcet as it was stentorian, pleasant as a banshee, joyful as a siren, resonant as it was mercurial, the music preordained by Reverend Ike stood in contrast to all expectations, its single up note uncanny to the crowd's ears, its persistence an offense to their composure. One of the crowd members, an old man who'd lost his wife and daughter to the Red Shirts during the last days of Reconstruction, said it must be the tornado siren in the far outskirts of West Jackson. Another of the crowd members, a young girl who devotedly kept track of the National Urban League's broadcasts from Strivers Row in Harlem, said it must be a wireless catching the signal from KRQ in New Orleans. None of the crowd was right, but one thing was for certain. The sound of God begat the fear of God.

With notably vaudevillian theatrics—one of Zinnerman's descendants would, years to come, work a routine on the Catskill circuit—Reverend Ike took a Quaker's hat he'd bartered years ago from a fellow traveler and let it be sallied hand to hand throughout the congregation. "The holy tithe is one of the most important sacraments decreed by God in heaven above," he said. "Please donate anything you can afford to do without, so that His word may be spread far and wide in this great land." It took less than ten minutes for the hat to grow lumpy with buffalo nickels, Lincoln pennies, and barber dimes. Around the same moment, unfortunately for Reverend Ike, fortunately for everyone else, the sound of God came to an abrupt end, replaced by tree branches snapping in half and the loud, tinny scream of a child.

The crowd rushed to the source. At a shady graveyard within shouting distance, they found a little boy spread unconscious on a bed of pine straw, his arm broken in two places, his face covered in scratch marks. A trumpet lay next to him. Let it not be said the common folk of the South lack a gift for deductive thought. Every gaze in the crowd shifted from the boy who'd obviously taken a spill from high up a tree, to the trumpet on the ground, to the man who'd obviously tried to swindle all of their hard-won money.

Such a picture of collective rage gave Reverend Ike ample grounds for concern. He put on a healthy smile. He let out a weak chuckle. Some five years back, he had seen a partner's skin peel from the bones of his legs and face and arms, the hot, black tar and duck feathers rendering him a monstrous skeleton. The waking nightmare that had plagued Reverend Ike since that day, those howls of pain so loud they rang in his teeth, that stench of burnt flesh so rank it made food a task, came back to him in the graveyard full of angry fathers, children, and mothers. His knees hit the soft earth at the foot of a headstone. His nails tore at a slab of granite cut by hand. Although his senses were so dull he could hardly read the grave's inscription—"William Jebediah Arnold, Great Soldier for the Confederacy, Loyal Friend, Honest Servant of Our Lord God, 1844-1868"—Reverend Ike clearly heard someone in the crowd say, "A man with such thieving fingers don't rightfully deserve them."

At the corner of Jefferson Street and 6th Avenue, one of the busiest junctions in all of Martinsville, Robert Johnson stood on the curb with his guitar at the ready. We have trouble imagining a scene that has been so degraded by legend. Not that we haven't smelt hot tamales steaming the pot of a roadside stand for a penny each, nor that we haven't seen children giving themselves frothy moustaches while drinking Coke floats at the local druggist. We certainly aren't strangers to the details of a southern street. Nevertheless, reflecting on a day of such mystery, renown, and scandal—the fabric of hearsay embroidered by the needlework of speculation—we find it hard to imagine our husband, who was always confident on stage, who was always calm under pressure, so not at himself that his hands shook with the all-overs.

"It's fine to have those jitters deep in your bones," Ike said to him, standing by his side. "Use it for the good. Channel that demon itch into your song."

Ike held his own guitar at the ready, as well, the fret angled in his whole hand and his finger stump tapping the baseboard. Only the third day of Robert's schooling at music but the first day of what Ike called trial by brimstone, this practice of "cutting heads," whereby two bluesmen on a busy street contend for the largest audience, was liable to give even the oldest hands sure enough reason for a wrinkly brow. Ike was about to start, but Robert interrupted him. "Mr. Ike, can I own something to you?"

"Don't preamble your intentions. Be out with it, son, be out with it."

"I'm not sure this is for me, being a musician and such like. Don't know I'm the right fit for a bluesman. Sometimes I think on quitting the whole of it. Just seems not really all that worth my trouble. I am not very good."

Ike gave the moment weight.

"Did you know there are a thousand little nigger boys in the Delta wanting to be where you are right now?" Ike said. "A *thousand* little nigger boys. They'd stand in line to be in your shoes. They'd give anything to be in your place. And how do you handle that?" Ike said. "With vanity. With hubris. With pity. I am not one to be a part of such things. Nuh-uh."

Robert could not find words.

"Don't you come to me with your 'Not the right fits' and

your 'Not worth my troubles,'" Ike said. "Expecting me to say, 'But Mr. Robert, you can't quit. The world's such a better place with your music in it. You're so good. Please don't quit!'" Ike said. "Guess what. One of those nigger Delta boys will gladly step up and take your place and be just as good if not better by half."

Ike let the moment sink.

"I'm sorry, Mr. Ike, I'm sorry. Don't have the faintest what was going on in my head. Really am thankful that—"

"Save that shit for later, fool." Ike could have taken the thought further, but he had already cut his first head. The chord of A-minor from his Kalamazoo hit Robert in the seat with the force of a hobnail boot. He did his best to catch up with Ike, but he only made a poor show of it. Robert lost himself in simple appreciation. Despite the lack of a pinkie finger on his strumming hand, Ike managed to play, with skill, with control, with ease, the full range of chords available on a six-string. Robert began to mimic the style. He used half of his fingers for the lead progression, but the other half were left with no purpose whatever. So, without pondering the technical significance and without grasping the historical consequence, Robert started playing the bass line with those other fingers. Two rhythms, one guitar. Who could have known the inspiration of genius would be as plain as idle hands?

Bear in mind his competition was no slouch neither. Although he allowed a moment for drop-jaw, Ike soon recovered and, rather than disrupt the chord progression, started to serve as back-up to Robert's lead. A crowd gathered round them. Three young women on their way to a Pageant of Birds, feathers papier-mâchéd to cardboard shaped like wings and strapped to their arms, hats styled like beaks painted orange and worn at a tilt on their heads, made eyes at those handsome men on guitar. Three schoolgirls giggled near each other's ears. Four housegirls fanned themselves in the cold. One old woman taking the long way to the First Presbyterian Church, her calloused hands snapping occasionally to the rhythm, her clenched mouth humming along to the beat, fumbled the makings of a cigarette. This most definitely could be taken for a scene within the ambit of our imagination.

The tune of their song constituted nothing more than a riff, so Robert did not expect Ike to introduce actual lyrics. He was mistaken. The words to the song that would one day be known as "Preaching Blues," their transcription cobbled from correspondence with our husband, still manage to elicit our pity for the confidence man dead these many years.

Although its meaning remains hidden from easy prospect, the parenthetical subtitle of "Preaching Blues" is the noteworthy phrase, "Up Jumped the Devil." Some say it was the songwriter's intention to include a final verse. At the moment Ike Zinnerman would have continued with more lyrics, however, a white man pushed his way through the audience with an expression on his face like as from the part of the Bible where God got angry. His straw boater and paper collar struck discordant amongst so many one-gallused farmers. The shine to his wingtips put folks in the mind of looking away. His damp cheeks and patrician temples grew as crimson as the skin of a Virginia peanut. The man stood his ground until everyone got curious about their feet.

"You there, with the gimp hand," he said, pointing at Ike, "have you ever been to Pascagoula?"

"What's that?"

"Address me as 'sir.'"

"What's that, sir?"

"It's a simple question, boy," he said, still pointing. "Have you ever been to Pascagoula?"

"No, sir." Ike allowed his profile, including the features of his face but also the gnarled stump on his hand, to be studied on by the white man. "I've heard of the town," he said, "but I've never had the pleasure."

The white man turned to Robert. "And you?"

"Me?"

"Did I stammer, boy?"

Robert told the man, "I never been to Pascagoula." Two years back, Robert had lost a substantial portion of his stake to a former member of the Copeland gang while playing seven-card stud in a Pascagoulan wharf house. "My playing partner's never been there either." Three months back, Ike had told Robert the story of how, prior to his arrival, he had spent time working at a paper-shell pecan plantation along the Pascagoula River. "Neither of us ever been to Pascagoula," Robert told the man.

Despite his obvious suspicions, each made all too apparent by the spray of tobacco gleet he left on the sidewalk, the white man, later identified as a descendant of General David E. Twiggs from Good Hope, Georgia, also identified as kinfolk to the family that owned the Singing River Pecan Plantation, walked away without further argument. Ike Zinnerman, the type of man who did not require to be forgiven but simply allowed himself to forget he'd committed a sin, held composure. What a picture he must have been to those listeners. The camber of Ike's delicate cheekbones, we know from a schoolteacher who to this day owns the calico housedress she wore that afternoon, caught sunshine at much the high angle. His eyelids bore no wrinkles. His temples kept dry of sweat. The half twist to his lips on just one side, we know from a seamstress whose drawn cheeks still get color at the memory eighty years afterwards, gave the impression of such imperturbable charm. No one ever said fallen angels are not beautiful.

William Jebediah Arnold joined the Provisional Army of the Confederate States following the Second Conscription Act of September 27, 1862. Ordnance Sergeant in the Army of Mississippi even after the surrender of the Vicksburg Campaign, he was known throughout the Western theater as one of the staunchest proponents of the white man's supremacy over the black man. His acrimony was matched only by his obstinacy. Given as much, William Jebediah Arnold, who succumbed after a rusty nail in the ankle left him with a bad case of lockjaw, most likely took pleasure from his special place in hell when on October 24, 1929, the historical date of our country's economic downfall, one of the "damn colored things" set free by the war had his pinkie finger cut from his hand six feet above the Ordnance Sergeant's corporal remains.

The instrument for the finger's removal was an old pair of barbed-wire clippers. Each of the dull blades let out shrieks almost human in pitch as somebody from the crowd took good measure of their utility. One man tackled Reverend Ike to the soggy ground. Another man snatched hold of the imposter's arm.

"Start with the little one first," a mother of twelve said from the back. "Make sure he don't go into a spell."

“Don’t let his thumb slip away,” a sister of eight said from farther back. “Their ashes bring a blessing on the soul.”

Reverend Ike could just barely discern, what with the poor vantage on his wet behind, a group of women taking care of the boy who’d fallen out of the tree. They were patting his cheek to bring him to consciousness. They were brushing dirt from the scrape on his forehead. They were lifting his body to save him the brutal witness. That was the reason why Reverend Ike was so overcome with relief—the boy was okay, at least, the boy was okay—even as the clippers began to pulverize his finger’s bone, tissue, and skin.

The relief did not keep for very long. Blood drenching the length of his arm, metal working its way into flesh, bone crunching to bits at the joint, Reverend Ike could only comprehend, soon enough, a pain beyond this kingdom on earth. He was very near to falling into a blackout when the first stone of hail struck the cemetery.

Despite their regular attention to meteorological activity, the people in the crowd, most of whom were farmers reliant on rain for their crops, had never seen balls of ice fall from the sky. Hailstorms are rare in Mississippi. What might should have made up for such pluralistic ignorance was the crowd’s extensive knowledge of all biblical phenomena. In their prayer books they had seen Moses parting the Red Sea to escape the Egyptians. They had been told sermons of the bush that was not consumed by flames. They had been shown illustrations of the sun and moon occupying the same sky. From their church pews they had heard tales of Noah protecting all the creatures on earth against a Great Flood. The meaning of tonight’s occurrence was obvious to everyone in the crowd. Heaven had frozen over.

During the initial welter of the hailstorm, its stones larger than acorns but smaller than eggs, its intensity high at first but slackening by the minute, Reverend Ike slipped away from the crowd of people, whose eyes were still gaping at the night sky. He chose the greater darkness of a bog. Across from the cemetery, some three hundred yards towards where the sun had set, lay a canebrake made deeper than usual by the past month's winter freshets. Reverend Ike dove towards the water but instead hit the muddy bank, his body sliding to a halt, comparable to a baseballist, less than a yard from the dark pool.

Most of the dirt found in the lowlands of Mississippi is called "buckshot" because of the bits of clay spread all throughout it. The clay makes the dirt as tacky as cake batter. It took less than a minute of flailing his arms and rolling on his back and whipping his legs for Reverend Ike to become an indistinguishable lump on the ground. He stayed completely still for the entire night. Never once did he lift his head to shoo away the opossum sniffing at his crotch. Never once did he move his leg to get rid of the leech sticking itself to his calf.

At dawn, not having heard the search party for a good many hours, Reverend Ike raised himself from the bank of the canebrake and walked towards the first light of a cold morning. He wouldn't have known that across the country decimal points on ticker tape were steadily creeping to the farthest left. He wouldn't have thought that around the world businessmen were lipping the bitter steel of their pocket revolvers. On October 25, 1929, little more than a sleepless night after stock markets at last hit bottom, the shell of dried mud, twigs, and grubby mulch covering Reverend Ike's body became more of a patchwork with each of his painful steps forward.

⁂

During summer months, the staff members of the Emerald Slipper would form a line in front of the outhouse each and every Tuesday. Calletta Craft required her employees to take a regular bath. During winter months, though, she allowed for the more lenient schedule of every other Tuesday. “Sweat cleans you almost the same as water,” she was wont to say, “but nothing warms a man like the smell of cunt.”

Another thing Callie was wont to say was that anybody who lived under the Emerald Slipper’s roof was considered a member of its staff. So, naturally, begrudgingly, timidly, Robert and Ike once again found themselves standing in line on the third day of the week, their red union suits buttoned at the ass in consideration of the upstairs girls, their breath unseasonably evident in the nip of an early April morning. The bathhouse contained two porcelain tubs, and the washbasin provided hunks of black soap. Whatever their annoyance at the routine of Callie’s requirement, Ike and Robert always managed to take pleasure in the luxury of such apparatus for hygiene, the beautiful claw feet adorning each of the tubs, the specks of wheat germ dashed throughout the soap.

“Today we’re going to practice some more on the piano,” Ike said as he lowered his body into the cool water. “I want you knowing it backwards and forwards.”

Robert dunked his head and returned for breath. “I about know it backwards and forwards already.”

Since Ike’s arrival five months ago, Robert had been training with him not only on how to improve his skills at the guitar but also on how to refine his grasp of music in general. Ike had taught Robert the rudiments of Pythagorean theory relative to the scale progression of chords. He tied a handkerchief around Robert's eyes and had him play blind. He dribbled hot paraffin into Robert's ears and had him play deaf. Ike had even shown Robert how to use harmonic analysis to play certain songs with nothing but his teeth. It would be near about forty years before another guitarist would make the same technique famous.

"One thing I want you to learn." Ike stood from the water and reached for his sackcloth towel. "Anything you can play on the piano, you can play on the guitar."

For a brief moment, as he dried every cranny of his parts and as he stepped into each leg of his union suit, Robert felt an eerie sense of the repetition in life, what he'd once heard an Acadian call *déjà vu*, as though he were being taught a lesson over and over by some higher authority. He liked to have sworn he'd heard those exact same words before today. Outside, walking back to the house, Robert erased the heebie-jeebies from his mind and started the process of preparing to play music. He had to concentrate. He had to clarify. He had to calibrate. The player piano in the lobby of the Emerald Slipper was an Aeolian Themodist gotten on the cheap for its obsolescence. On arrival, after Robert had agreed to the mentorship but before the actual training had begun for real, Ike had taken it on himself not only to fix the thing but also to modify it for manual play. The piano was stained with lampblack from its years at a saloon in the hill country of Georgia, upright, sturdy, tuned close as possible to perfection given it was so up in years, polished, spit-shined, dusted, and, right as when Ike and Robert entered the lobby from their baths, being played by the very same white man who, three weeks earlier, had interrupted their play on the street corner.

"My grandfather, the illustrious General David E. Twiggs, was a hero of the War of 1812 and the Mexican-American War." He looked only at the sheet notes. "David E. Twiggs was one of the oldest generals on either side during the War of Northern Aggression." He never once looked at Robert and Ike. "General Twiggs, mind you now, appreciated music of quality."

The white man played exceptionally well. Even though neither Ike nor Robert could recognize the piece, we know from the occasions when our husband would hum it, in the middle of bad sleep, on a drunken tear, at any time of full silence, that it was a movement from Beethoven's Symphony No. 9. He played for what seemed an eternity. At last, twisting in his seat and reaching for a key, the white man hit a dead note. He tapped the key a few more times without any gain. *Plink, plink.* The white man said, "Looks as if one of your keys is broken," as he turned to stare through Ike. *Plinkety, plink, plink.*

Robert did not notice the three other men step through the doorway at his back, but he did notice them grab Ike from behind and wrap a piano wire around his neck. One of the men made Robert see constellations by knocking him in the jaw something awful. On the floor, Robert watched the white man stand from the piano bench and walk towards the black man writhing desperately to free himself.

"That ring you took from my family's house use to belong to General Twiggs," the white man said. "It was given to him by the honorable President Jefferson Davis himself."

In a series of entries from the white man's journal, a helpful item we bought from an estate sale after his family went bankrupt, the grandson of General David E. Twiggs described the reasons for his pursuit of Ike Zinnerman and the measures by which he eventually found him. Ike had taken a position in Pascagoula as a crate packer at the Singing River Pecan Plantation owned and operated by a favorite uncle of the white man. One evening a few weeks into his tenure, having ferreted the information from a cook peculiarly subject to his wiles, Ike snuck into the house and stole the family heirlooms, a particular item of which being a gold ring engraved, "Distinguished Gentleman from the Confederated States of America." The white man spent months traveling through the South in search of the black man he had been told in back-cap was missing a pinkie finger. One day on the downtown streets of Martinsville, close to quitting his enterprise due to its lack of progress, the white man happened across a guitar player with only four fingers to his strumming hand.

"I got no idea what you're talking about." Ike could only yell with difficulty. The blood from the piano wire matched near perfect the red of his union suit. "I'm telling you I got no idea what goddamn ring you're talking about."

"That so," the white man said, "is it now?" He raised a gold ring to the light. "Suppose this found its way into your suitcase by accident."

The three other men tightened their grip on Ike's arms and repositioned the piano wire around his neck. They kicked his legs from under him and dragged his body towards the door. Despite the palpable hurt of Ike's attitude, his face dissolving to ashy, his neck delineated with veins, he looked in Robert's direction and said, "Tell my son I'm sorry about the tree." Robert hadn't the faintest. He would recall those words, however, for the rest of his short life.

The events that happened next were witnessed from a variety of perspectives. Robert Johnson watched from the porch, where he had managed to crawl even with his senses yet fully intact, as the white men chose a strong tree in the front yard. The upstairs girls huddled together, crying and whispering and praying, as the white men strung a rope. Calletta Craft watched from her bedroom window, where she clenched a sweaty wad of bluebacks offered for her cooperation, as the white men bound Ike's hands and feet together. The last perspective belonged to a seller of tintypes. On his way to the Emerald Slipper for a visit with his favorite girl, the tintypist saw the events proceeding forth at an honest distance, their meaning obvious to him because his father had gotten similar treatment from municipal deputies ten years ago. He set up his equipment just in time. The ambrotype image of Reverend Ike Zinnerman hanging from the branch of a live oak, piano wire laced around his neck beneath layers of thick rope, his tongue a purple extrusion, his eyes round scarlet bulbs, two trickles of blood threaded from each ear down his neck, would later appear as a fold-out on pages 32-33 of *Life* Magazine's September 13, 1964, issue, beneath the caption, "Unknown Negro man hung by angry mob in Martinsville, Mississippi." Its title was *Untitled.*

“Stop Breakin’ Down Blues”

We received proof of his life less than a month after his death. In late September of 1938, a period of days on record as the hottest in state history, our memories of Robert Johnson had begun to entangle themselves with the sensations of our skin gamy in the joints and our dresses glued to sweaty thighs. We could hear him in the symphonic trickle of riverbeds parched by crop storms. We could smell him in the effluvial perfume of tomatoes fallen to decay. At each of our homes in towns scattered throughout the Delta—Tabitha lived in Tutwiler, Helena lived in Yazoo—all six of us distracted ourselves from both the heat and his memory by snapping peas on the porch, by beating dirt from rugs in the yard, by scrubbing laundry with lye in the washroom. Our chores were interrupted when the postman arrived at each of our homes carrying parcels that bore each of our names. We immediately recognized our husband’s serpentine scrawl.

Each of the packages contained a single photograph. Such content, sunk in an oversized box and swaddled in cornhusks, rang peculiar to us for more than one reason. We had never known Robert Johnson to pose for a picture, as he had lived in deathly fear of having his image put on film. We had never seen him wear so dapper a suit. We had never known him to sit as straight. We had never seen him smiling such a careless grin.

Most perplexing of all, we received the photograph two whole weeks after our husband's murder.

Was he forced to take the picture against his will, we ask ourselves to this day, or did some doppelganger pose in front of the gargantuan Kodak? Did he mail the package prior to his death? If so, did the postal service delay the delivery until afterwards? Could it be possible that Robert Johnson, dead but a fortnight, was still alive?

The only evidence available for study was the portrait we hold now in our trembling hands. Even to this day it works the hypnotist's machinations on our fading memories of Robert Johnson. The face transposed onto heavy card stock, all but disfigured by various tricks of light, bears the veronica of the man we helped shave every morning. His left eyelid hangs half-mast from the untreatable cataract. His left ear droops doggish from a childhood fishing accident. Sepia-tinted shadows morph our late husband's chin and jaw into those of someone else, but his nose, forehead, and mouth stay true to the originals that once provided our lips a place to rest.

Even more so than his facial features, however, we recognize Robert Johnson's long, delicate, spidery hands. They could play the blues like no other. They could invigorate our bodies like no one else. The sight of them coiled around his Gibson L-1 remind us, now as well as then, of our husband's fingers kudzuing along our spines, of his palms feeling for fever on our brows. They remind us of his knuckles kneading knots in our shoulders, of his nails soothing an itch we'll never be able to reach. Ever since the day we received the photograph, those hands have caused our husband's ghost to rise from the monochromatic gloom.

We have spent the past seventy years trying to fathom the circumstances of the photograph. Our imaginations have realized the occasion of its capture. We have built dioramas of the Hooks Bros. Studio, whose insignia marks the bottom left corner. We have sketched storyboards of the day our husband was photographed in Memphis, Tennessee. We have envisioned him sauntering down Front Street in close-up and entering a Cotton Row four-story from a high angle. We have created a montage of him quibbling over the price and bragging he just released a record and shaking the hand of the photographer. We have edited his last words for content. "Give me an extra six copies," he tells the gentleman who operated aperture and lens. "There's a few ladies I want to make proud."

The picture has framed our lives. It has accompanied us to job interviews and to counseling sessions. It has brought us luck before the title match, during college exams, and after the flop. It has comforted us in the waiting room. It has bourn witness as we gave our children away in marriage, as we soaped our ring fingers slick and welcomed other men into our beds, as we cleared a place setting for one, called collect on Easter Sunday, and lied about tickles in our throats.

Over the years since his death, as our late husband's music grew famous and as his life became myth, streetwise historians and plainclothes reporters have ransacked the traveling-man motels, the nickel-and-ten recording shacks, and the Highway 61 juke joints of Mississippi in the hope they might stumble across visual verification of Robert Johnson's existence. They have questioned relatives by blood. They have searched premises without warrants. It wasn't until 1989, over fifty years after his death and almost eighty years after his birth, that the entire world was finally given tangible proof of our husband's life, its dimensions eight by ten inches.

A man named Stephen LaVere, whose name and actions we know from numerous articles published in recent years, made the discovery while interviewing our husband's half-sister, Carrie Thompson. "A snapshot of my brother? Well, let's take a look-see," we imagine she said to the nice man asking about little Robbie. "I've got some of his things stored away in the closet." She spent ten minutes rifling through an old cedar chest, its contents a veritable gold mine for any blues historian. Mr. LaVere's pupils dilated to the size of mercury dimes as Mrs. Thompson removed two photographs, one small and one large, that would earn both of them thousands of dollars in the years to come. The first photograph, which would later be known as the "Photo-Booth Self-Portrait," portrayed Robert Johnson posing with his guitar, an unlit Chesterfield hanging from his lip. The second photograph, which would later be known as the "Hooks Bros. Studio Portrait," was the very one we received two weeks after our husband's death.

We, the wives of Robert Johnson, were never questioned by historians or reporters. We, the inheritors of his legacy, were never asked about the truth of our late husband's life. Our existence has been glossed by time. If only someone had read between the lines of history and found our names scribbled in the margins, they would have discovered a photograph of the legendary blues singer much sooner than 1989. If only someone had knocked on our doors sometime over the past seventy years, they would have found his portrait on the mantle, or plastered inside an album, or atop the bedside table, or sandwiched within a cookbook. Claudette, the archivist, kept it filed under V for

Visual. Betty, the drunk, kept it crumpled in her back pocket. If only someone had searched for our existence as fervently as they did that of our husband, we would have shown them the photograph we received on a series of afternoons in 1938. We would have flipped it over and read them the inscription our husband wrote to each of us seventy years ago. "To my one and only love," it reads in his beautiful cursive. "Yours forever, RJ."

CHAPTER FOUR

The cocker spaniel had been dead for rough on a fortnight. From its visible eye seeped heavy pus reflecting the color of an early spring sunset. Along the Zoysia grass ran streaks of blood left flaky by the Alabama heat. From its lockjaw snout drooped a shrunken tongue going spotty with iridescent blowflies. Our husband took a long stretch of his hamstring over the dead dog without even noticing the dead puppy just begun to crown from its hind parts.

His indifference came natural to him. Dogs are always getting shot and snake-bit and rurnt over in the South. That's how our children learn of death.

Since daybreak, when he arrived in the Port City on the 5:48 of the northwest feeder line, Robert Johnson had been wandering among the body parts of giants. He ducked under the fingers and palms of two hands each the size of a flatbed truck. He stared into an eye bigger than his head and he listened by an ear wider than his shoulders and he sniffed at a nose longer than his arm. He sidestepped a tongue protruding like a cowcatcher and bumped into a foot as obtrusive as a hayrick. Across the county line, spread throughout an overgrown cow pasture whose location was kept secret from mischievous pickaninnies, the fleet of carnival floats lay in wait for their last parade along the streets of Mobile, Alabama. Tomorrow was

Shrove Tuesday.

Robert should have known the invitation had something to do with Mardi Gras. Two weeks earlier, a letter had arrived by private post at one of our homes, we prefer not to specify which, along with a certified cashier's check for twenty dollars, a tuxedo, and a travel voucher on the best railcar for those of color. "Dear Robert Johnson the Guitarist, Your musical services are requested on Tuesday, March 5, 1935, in Alabama's grandest and finest city of Mobile." The words in Egyptian dye were written on paper of Eucalyptus bond. "The first payment of $100 shall be rendered upon arrival. The second payment of $100 shall owe to satisfactory completion of duties." What's more, the invitation, signed with elegant penmanship by "Shadrach Farnsworth III, Esq." and sealed by impressed wax with the insignia "O of M," included an address, 593 Plank Road, as well as directions on how to get there by foot or by cab from Terminal Station.

Around noon, Robert reached the antebellum estate located at 593 Plank Road in a part of town known as Spring Hill, a residential neighborhood of Mobile's wealthiest and oldest families. The big house of the estate typified the city's history through a diverse range of architectural style. Some of its many features in the French Colonial mode included cornices narrow but long and white stucco molded to brick. Spanish influence could be found in its low-pitched roof with shingles of motley earth tone. The second-floor gallery, designed with an eye to the Georgian Colonial homes in northern cities, studded with Oriel windows left slightly uneven by a British carpenter's hand, and extended fully around three sides of the Post-Colonial main structure, was distinguished by the ornamental ironwork of its balustrades, one of the few artistic triumphs from the days of slavery, the metal's African-American patterns of Christianity depicting seraphim and cherubim in flight above the throne of a benevolent God. Roman classicism could be noted in the house's arched doorway with distinct panels. Over almost the entirety of the front yard, an expansive Greek peristyle of twenty-five Ionic, Corinthian, and Doric columns, each situated atop a marble stylobate and plastered with the molasses treatment, brought conclusion to 593 Plank Road's scattershot influences of nationality. Mobile wasn't known as the City of Five Flags by mere happenchance.

It almost seemed beyond our husband's measure of purpose, considering the yard rooster presently crowing not towards the house but rather with direction at the road twenty paces back, for Robert to pull the gold braid hanging from the entrance bell. The door opened before he had time to give it second thought. An index finger of some arthritic hand motioned him forward with a pop of its joint. The shadows inside the deep foyer restrained him to the dark at first step. Robert pondered the myriad parlor rooms of the plantation house that would one day come under jurisdiction of the Southern Alabama Historical and Cultural Preservation Society as an elderly servant woman in a pristine red paisley smock guided Robert to his destination in the eastern wing. He walked across twelve-inch-wide floor boarding of superior yellow pine, and he walked beneath ceilings at least twenty feet high over the wainscot. From the kitchen, somewhere out of sight around the corner, Robert noticed the vinegar scent of corn hominy grits in their process. In the living room, mute behind tall French doors of pane glass, Robert noticed a portraiture of cotton river packets done with oil paint. The house woman led him up a curved stairway.

"You stay in here up 'til Mr. Farnsworth makes time for you," she said while leading Robert into a study. They were the first words, he realized, she had spoken as of yet. "I am to tell you"—the old woman paused for quotation—"'to make yourself at home.'"

All too alone on the house servant's departure, Robert calmed his nerves by busying himself about the study, looking at a totem of delicate china painting strung up the crimson wall, fingering a set of pewter utensils for mail atop the desk of fine mahogany wood. The plush marks of his feet looked as dance steps against the oriental rug. On the far side of the room, where his nervous movement finally made the riffle to a brief standstill, Robert looked out a window that gave unto the backfields. Live oaks, thick as Webster's glossary, drooped with Spanish moss. Low fog, dense as Shakespeare's theatricals, rolled through Tung trees. The temperature seemed chill even for springtime. Along the hedge border ran white bay, inkberry, and wild olive shrubs, in addition to one particular strand Robert could not identify. Beyond the hedge line stood a group of farmhands surrounding a copper pot, heaps of wood, a chimney pit, and stacks of kettles, a scene Robert knew to be the making of cane syrup. Cypress smoke rose above a flowering dogwood.

"You look into the fiery mouth of the devil and all you get is a glimpse at his tonsils."

Shadrach Farnsworth III, Esq., took pride in assertions that were partial to scrutiny—they'd scan as either Old Testament proverb, Norse rune, Jim Dandy palaver, or Zen koan if put to a poet's eye—though we unfortunately no longer hobby ourselves with samplers. Farnsworth had by the looks of it been standing in the doorway for some time, watching at how Robert felt about the prospect of the backfield. The owner of the estate was on the green side of sixty. He wore a two-button suit of natural fabric in the raw, blackseed cotton showing its yellow tint along with specks of twiggy brown, as though he were a piece of toast that had fallen buttered side to the floor. His hair was white and his face was pink, both colors having been there from birth.

Member of the affluent Bankhead family on his mother's side, Farnsworth had given his most famous niece considerable fatherly attention during her childhood years, and nowadays, even despite said niece's reputation in the picture business, he was known as the only family member to be "tolerant of Tallulah." His ends were as significant as his means. Farnsworth owned 8,000 acres of cotton farmland throughout the Black Belt, was on the general council for Christ Church, was on the charity board of Bellingrath Gardens, and had co-sponsored the Cotton Control Act of the New Deal. He professed to have descended from one of the Cassette girls, twenty-three orphans from Quebec who'd arrived at Mobile Port in 1704 on the *Pelican* with only their namesake luggage, in particular the one of them said to have been "coy and hard to please." We can neither prove nor disprove the claim.

"Mr. Johnson, I presume," Farnsworth said, "or do you prefer Mr. Spencer?"

Prior to first hearing this story, less than a few weeks after the events to follow, we had always believed nobody but us knew of the latter name, but during the time of its occurrence, Robert's thoughts clung far more greedily to the title of "Mister." Anybody not so full up on himself would have considered it cause for suspicion.

"Johnson's fine."

Farnsworth wrapped his large, broad hand around Robert's thin, long fingers, pumped four times, and motioned for Robert to hitch quarters on the settee, its cushions upholstered in sateen bands of alternating gray shade. The big man said, "Can I get you a drink, Mr. Johnson?"

"That's all right, thank you."

"Have some currant brandy." Farnsworth commenced a rattling of glassware and carafes at a bar across the room, his back in obstruction of Robert's view to the procedure. "I have it imported special from Warsaw."

"Appreciative."

Robert accepted the snifter of currant brandy. Every one of us likes to think that, knowing our husband's limited expertise in liquor of the fancy sort, Robert must have considered it a "recent vintage." The drink was as sweet and thick as sherry reduced over a low flame. Its coloring had a purplish tint. Farnsworth gulped at something brown.

"I supposed your mind is reeling at the fishhook of a question: 'Why am I here?' " Behind the desk, sitting down in a flat-wing chair, Farnsworth's large buttocks, fed copious on Southern cooking since birth, gave a run at the leather's tensility. "Pardon the metaphor. I don't mean to imply, well, that you took the bait."

"Don't give it any mind," Robert said. "I enjoy a good metaphor."

Although the settee, a type of sofa he'd once heard called a fainting couch, sat close to the floor, Robert could still observe the business going on out the window. He knew how to make syrup. Years ago, during his stint at the Abbay & Leatherman plantation, he'd taken a machete to enough sugar cane that his fingers could sweeten coffee with one dip. Those were the old days. That was the old him. What a sight he would make to the folks from his way back, our husband told us he was thinking at the time, what a picture he would be to the world from his long ago. Robert getting shown around the house, Robert being called "Mister" by a white man, Robert having his drink served to him. He was so caught up in his own revelries he almost didn't catch the real story of his invitation. Farnsworth had said something about a ball for Mardi Gras with a whereabouts that was of the utmost secrecy, Robert could remember, as well as something about a Mystic Society the name of which was known but to members only. Did Robert follow? Not a lick. He said, "So why am I here?"

"We need a musician."

"A musician."

"Consider a ball without music. That'd be akin to a pussy without pussy juice," Farnsworth said, the account of which never fails to compel us to take back up our stitchwork. He said, "Ever tried to make sex to a pussy without pussy juice? Rub a man sore to the bone."

Robert had never heard such language from a person in high authority. The currant brandy did little to settle the unease those words brought to his stomach. He felt a mizzy in his gut. Robert set the half empty snifter on the table beside the fainting couch.

"The Farnsworth land used to belong to the Creek Indians. Did you know that? Very interesting people, the Creek Indians, very interesting people. Believed in the occult."

"The what?"

"Magic. They were known to make a special concoction, what they called the black drink, from a species of shrub native to these parts. The Cassina bush. You may know it as the Yaupon."

"Black drink."

"Supposed to clear the mind. Warriors drank it when they prepared for war. Headmen drank it when they assembled in council. The black drink acted as just a mild nerve sedative. Understood? The herbal essence required whole lots of dilution."

It took concentration for Robert to lift his drink from the table. He tried a hard gaze into the snifter, where color of his reflection was indistinguishable from that of the liquid, but he could not stare with true aim.

"Drink up, boy," said Farnsworth. "We don't got all day."

Robert swatted at a lightning bug, unusual for this early in the afternoon, that had somehow gotten into the house. He stood with attention like a soldier, strolled to the window like a widow, and saw through eyes like a drunkard. His feet stuck to the floor. His focus drew towards the yard. The cane syrup burbling in its hot copper pot over a trench of coals, our husband noticed just prior to dropping his snifter, would thicken too much if somebody didn't stir it soon.

On January 31, 1830—over a century after the first Mardi Gras celebration took place in what would become the United States at a French settlement called Twenty-Seven Mile Bluff in what would become Mobile—Michael Krafft, a Dutch cotton broker formerly of Pennsylvania, celebrated *Boeuf Gras* with friends at a restaurant in the Port City's downtown district. The revelers stumbled into the streets near midnight. According to town gossip that has since become historical record, Krafft led his drunken entourage to a hardware store, where they borrowed cowbells, rakes, hoes, and shovels without consent, and paraded along the shell-top, wide-lane thoroughfares of Mobile, Alabama. The first Mystic Society of Mardi Gras would thenceforth be called the Cowbellion de Rakin Society. Over the decades to follow, many other Mystic Societies were organized by the citizens of Mobile, including the Order of Myths, Comic Cowboys, Strikers Independent Society, the Infant Mystics, Mobile Women Mystics, Tea Drinkers, and the Order of Doves, Mobile's first black society. It remains unknown, then as now, which of them hired our husband to play his music at their ball, drugged him to maintain their secrecy, transported his unconscious body to a clandestine site, and poured a bucket of water onto his slumberous head.

The shock of moisture woke Robert in a room lit only by candles. He got a hang on himself. The walls of the room were built with the kind of brick cooked in home furnaces, and the air of the room was rank with the kind of givy that resides in home basements. Robert lay on a cot with a hay mattress but no sheets. He placed his feet on the concrete floor. The only other furniture in the room was a chair that held a pile of what looked to be his clothes. At the same instant Robert realized he was dressed in the tuxedo that had come with his invitation, he discerned with a start the figure of Farnsworth standing in a distant corner of the room. The candlelight gave him a ghoulish complexion as he said, "How does it fit?"

Robert assessed the tuxedo, running his hands down the

curved lapels, tracing the line of its hem, sticking two fingers inside the waistband. "Perfect," he said.

"I should expect so."

"What am I doing here?"

"Fulfilling your contractual services." Farnsworth, dressed in a tuxedo of his own, came a foot or two closer. "In your pocket you'll find one hundred dollars, the other hundred to be delivered at the evening's conclusion."

"It's evening right now?"

"Tuesday evening."

"I been out a day and a half?"

"Guess I was a little careless with the proportions," Farnsworth said. "You'll have to wear this throughout the night."

Farnsworth tossed a white object onto the mattress. On inspection, Robert saw that it was a mask, the nose, forehead, and cheeks made of a rubbery plaster, some twine run around the back, and, most striking, a hole at the mouth but none at the eyes. Robert asked how he was supposed to see anything.

"That's the point, dummy."

"How am I supposed to see the guitar strings?"

"From what I've heard," Farnsworth said, "you won't have to."

After a moment's hesitation, Farnsworth said it was about time for them to get. He wanted to know if our husband needed help. Robert still felt pale, but he could manage. Farnsworth stood Robert from the cot and led him out of the damp room. They went through a succession of doors: metal ones, wooden ones, metal ones with wooden panels, one with a peephole, one with a glass window, granite ones, brick ones, marble ones, and one that didn't have a knob. Prior to the last of the doors,

Farnsworth covered his face with a harlequin mask, yellow diamonds beneath and above the eyes, purple outline of lips over the impression of a mouth. He nodded for Robert to put on his own. The mask fit a tad snug. Robert heard the door open with a cavernous groan and was led into a room with plenty of echo. He could tell by the chorus of whispers there were hundreds of people watching him, exactly as does the shy introvert, but this could not be judged a repression of the ego when confronted with society. We have seen, it is true, many a therapist. Robert was taken onto a stage, placed in a chair, and given his own guitar.

"You know what to do," Farnsworth said into his ear as the crowd's volume rose to a din. "Put the fear of God in us."

At first, Robert played a few easy numbers, ones they would have heard—some old ragtime, the latest Cole Porter, a waltz number, some polka, the latest Bing Crosby—until he was sufficiently warmed up to give them his own catalog. We often asked him what he heard from the audience, but he was never able to provide us with an answer. Our husband was stone deaf to many like situations. "Would you start a fire, honey—it's getting cold tonight?" or "Would you toss another log, dear, the flames are going down?" "How about a kiss before bed?" "Did I tell you what happened at the store the other day?" and "Why didn't you tell me you wouldn't be home last night?" "I missed you." "I love you." "I sensed you." "I hear you." "Do you ever think of me when you're on stage?" and "I want to hear you play" and "Tell me just one thing. Is there somebody else?" Over the years of marriage, despite our efforts to change him for the better, every one of us grew accustomed to this tendency in our husband. There was nothing to hear but himself.

Robert concluded his set at the masquerade with songs that easily did the job, "Hellhound on my Trail," "Me and the Devil Blues," and "Cross Road Blues," each of which he played a huckleberry above the persimmon. He laid the guitar in his lap to signify the end. Somebody gripped him at the collar and guided him away from the stage. The door opened with its peculiar moan.

On his departure from the ball, Robert left not only the mysteries of who was in the audience, which masks did they wear, how were they dressed, where was the ball held, and what theme decorated the room, all questions that had to be answered by sight, but also whether it was a buck party or hen party or both, what mood dominated the crowd, did they enjoy his music or were they unimpressed, and why was everything such a big damn secret, questions that could have been at least partially answered by sound. Someone pushed Robert forward, the door closing behind him. Shadrach Farnsworth III, Esq., remained a purveyor of the epigram to their very last communication.

"This is going to hurt you more than it hurts me."

Weeks later, as Robert recounted the events to each of us, first one, then another, so forth, as Robert reached this moment within the story, all of our hearts beat us to the punch. Those risen knuckles cracked hard against Robert's temple with shocking clout for a planter gone to seed. It took another one to the jaw before he finally went unconscious.

Robert came back to his senses in a victory garden that had been overrun since the war. On a thicket of wildflowers, azalea and wisteria and lilac and camellia, he lay without moving so much as an eyelash, still dressed to the nines in his tuxedo. Artificial stars bloomed above his dizzy head. Robert knew by those fireworks a parade must be nearby. The very first thing he did was check for the $200. He found it wadded into the pocket of his coat. The next thing he did was look for his guitar. He saw it leaning against a picket fencepost.

Although cold as bringer and dark as flugins, the night was still hours upon hours from moondown. The sky certainly did appear as though it were about to rain tadpoles. Robert decided to locomote towards the parade. Colorful petals falling from his black-and-white garb, knots at his temple and jaw, twigs in his hair and collar, dirty face reflected in his glossy patent-leather shoes, he must have looked off his kerzip to any onlookers from where he found himself, Africatown, a settlement originally started in 1860 by the illegal cargo from a schooner, *Clotilde,* whose particular trade had been outlawed in America since 1808. Robert used the bursts of fireworks as celestial navigation to guide him south towards the downtown district. People who lived near what used to be called the Mobile & Ohio Railroad Yards might have taken him for a ringmaster on leave from the Barnum & Bailey. Folks who worked the late shift at what would soon be known as the Alabama State Docks could have thought him the telekinetic wunderkind from last week's *Ripley's Believe It or Not!* He had something of the showman about him. On Lipscomb Street, withstanding such conjecture, a few residents of the neighborhood had a very specific reaction to the presence of our husband. The brothel seemed to be going at full tilt. Drunken men still wearing carnival regalia wandered in and out of the house with curtains made of red broadcloth, and sober women half naked in flapper dresses stood on and off the front sidewalk with their attributes at display. One of the working girls, her thighs a creamy brown beneath the quarter moon, her cleavage tones of pink under shade of the house, saw Robert coming her way.

"Look at the gentleman coming my way," she said. "I'd give a discount to be with a real gentleman. Can I be of interest?"

Robert paused in front of the house, not staring at the sequins of her headband, not staring at the polish of her toenails. Can't say it surprises us one bit. The back seam of our panty hose could run him off the road. The front snap of our halter tops could stop him in his tracks. All we need to know is that he turned down her offer, which he did with a bow, placing one hand at his waist, the other at his lower back, bending his torso all the way forward. His silhouette along the ground shrunk temporarily with the maneuver.

"Just like I said, a gentleman, but he's walking away," the working girl said as Robert walked away. "You come back and see me, gentleman. You come back and see me anytime."

Over the next dozen or so blocks, Robert watched the city's progression from residential to commercial infrastructure, getting an eyeful of such Mobile landmarks as the Old Register Building, Madame le Vert's House, and the Old Federal Building, though never once did Robert stop wondering, he would later tell us, if it really and truly were possible for him to be that type of man, a real man, a true man, our man. He passed beside Bienville Square on its eastern border. It reminded him most all of a cemetery with spirits run amok from their graves. Children were playing hide-and-seek well past time for bed. At last, Robert reached a corner of Government Street, where the parade was rolling by Conception.

Our husband was back amongst company. Carnival goers done up in costumes of purple, green, and yellow danced their way down the street, tossing chocolate and vanilla Moon Pies to the eager crowds along the sidewalk. On either side of him, Robert was flanked by a clawhammer and a flyaway, both of whom already had rumbuds from weeks of excess drink. One man stood firing a pocket gun over his head. These people were pickled on gin, an op-ed staff writer for the *Mobile Register* would report the following week, but they kept their powder dry.

He was surrounded by the giants he had encountered outside the city. To his right, he recognized the circus clown pouting behind vast swaths of red acrylic paint. To his left, he recognized the court jester wincing at the enormous bells of a papier-mâché cap. Robert had to stoop under a marrote, round about the size of a cannon, passing slowly over the crowd. There were also some floats he hadn't noticed earlier. A green, scaly dragon was frozen in the attempt to whisk its tongue at the bushy, yellow tail of a lion. The heads of two minstrel performers in blackface made silent quiblets at one another on top of a coal wagon. On one of the largest floats stood a broken column, "The Pillar of Life," around which a man dressed as a fool chased a man dressed as a skeleton. "Folly" eventually defeated "Death." Robert was entranced by the sight until another of his senses took precedence.

He heard something next to him unnatural for this side of the earth. It was the whimper, high in pitch and low to ground, of a creature in pain. The sound became manifest as a tactile sensation when the cocker spaniel began to lick his palm.

Robert drew his hand back. Breathing got to be a struggle, and sweating became a mite too easy. There was no doubting he had already seen this dog earlier in the trip. Dead leaves clung to its coat of matted fur. Beneath its legs a runlet of urine tributized a steady flow of drool. Between its eyes a crust of gunk obstructed pupils rigid with dilation. Afterbirth fell in globules from its wagging tail. Poor thing must have come along when the parade floats were taken from their hideaway. It probably was pleasant for the dog to see a familiar face.

That was only the first of two ghosts Robert Johnson would encounter over the remaining three years of his life.

"Cross Road Blues"

On a dark night some years back, so goes the narration most everyone has heard told, a young man walked down a gravel road in the Mississippi countryside, satchel of clothes in one hand, roughhewn guitar in the other. Cotton fields to either side obscured the echo of his footsteps. Lightning bolts in the distance handled the placement of his shadow. It is at this point of the story, as the man came upon a crossroads, as the hour drew close to midnight, events vary depending on the teller. Some say he knelt down beneath a signpost writ with biblical verse rather than arrows of direction. Others say he took a seat on a boulder so large it could have only been put there by divine will. Despite any and all discrepancies, what happened next, the young man fiddling with his guitar, a cold finger tapping his shoulder, the offer of a bargain asking for his soul, has become more than mere story.

The legends of Robert Johnson have allowed us to map the darkest regions of his life. They have given a plot to his history and they have put a framework to his myth. In *Searching for Robert Johnson*, Peter Guralnick wrote, "Communication in the world in which Robert Johnson lived was almost exclusively oral, and although contacts were made and tales were told, the contacts were almost always tangential; the stories—while often maintaining a basis in fact—were in a sense as mythopoetic as those of the ancient Greeks." Clarence Postlethwaite, the famous biographer of Django Reinhardt, Edith Piaf, and Serge Gainsbourg, described Johnson in terms of that most significant of all American traits, self-invention, as tragic as Gatsby, as slippery as Sawyer, and as epic as Ahab. In *Robert Johnson: Lost and Found*, Barry Lee Pearson and Bill McCulloch wrote, "It's easy to get carried away, because blues-idiom poetry is fluid enough to accommodate multiple interpretations. And as we have seen, interpretation is often influenced more by what the reader brings to the reading than by what's there in the lyrics." Simon Marigold, who recently won a National Book Award for *Race Records: A Journey from Injustice to Justice with Accompanying Music*, referenced Johnson as an example of another American trait, self-destruction, calling him the type of man for whom success could only become eternal after death. "If Robert Johnson had not existed," Bruce Cook wrote in *Listen to the Blues*, "they would have to have invented him." We disagree. If Robert Johnson had not been invented, the passage should read, he would not have had reason to exist.

All of us can remember the day our husband gainsaid the usual versions of his encounter at the crossroads. It was during the first years of marriage. That was a time when Robert would make to whisper a confidence but instead leave our ears wet with kiss. That was also a time when he would sneak on his tiptoes from behind and ornament our necks with something fancy. One evening in our respective homes, as we giggled and wiped at our earlobes, as we blushed and fingered the necklaces, each of us found the gumption to ask Robert Johnson whether or not he had sold his soul to the devil.

"What does it matter whether or not it's true, play pretty?"

That was our husband's handle for us at times of bewilderment. Genius can't be obliged to keep straight of the little things. "Anything's true so long as people believe it."

Each of us asked him separately, in different chairs, in different hairstyles, in different dresses, in different light, what made people even start to think of it.

"I'll tell you one thing. Bluesmen hardly ever are known to think," he said, letting the contemplation distort his vision. "But I'll tell you another. We got something for the thoughtful."

At our insistence on the details, Robert told us how he had contributed to the make-believe of himself. His long absence and subsequent return to the blues circuit, those number of years pinching plugs of tobacco and pilfering pulls of whiskey in the hope of better understanding artistic abandon, led many to suspect devilment in his progression. Nobody could learn the guitar like that without somebody's help. Robert did not mention how he had gone to the woodshed for a time, bunking in a whorehouse, focusing on his trade, nor did he mention his short but crucial apprenticeship with Reverend Ike Zinnerman.

"So I told them, sure, the devil had a hand in it. What? Don't be looking at me like that," he said to us. Next, his mouth less than whisper distance to each of our ears, his breath hot against the pearls around our necks, our husband asked, "Don't you know anything can be improved with a lie, play pretty?"

Even during his lifetime, truth to tell, Robert Johnson's existence was more hearsay than daresay. Many people forget that legends are born from a lack of knowledge. Ever heard the story of how he took up with a midget woman for an entire month so as he could recuperate after a drunken stumble down a porch with a stump for stairs? False. The grass widow from

Decatur, herself named Midge, only had a clubfoot for disability, and Robert Johnson's stay with her, itself no more than two weeks, had to do with pneumonia. What about the one where Robert Johnson brought an entire crowd of people to tears with one of his songs? True. The song was called "Stop Breakin' Down Blues," and the venue was near Port Gibson. Have you ever heard he was the inspiration for a Tijuana bible's recurring character, The Golden Rule, whose catchphrase, "I give as good as I get," can be found scrawled on cathouse walls throughout the Baja Peninsula? Have you ever heard he was probed and prodded and pricked by green creatures with bulbous heads, sometimes said to hail from Ursa Major but other times said to be indigenous of the Milky Way, who had abducted him from the side of US Highway 66 as he hitchhiked near the outskirts of Roswell, New Mexico? False and false. How about the one where Robert Johnson married six different women, each of whom has spent her life in silent devotion to a man dead at such a young age? Only the truest things in creation are allowed to be long for this world.

"Did Robert really love? Yes, like a hobo loves a train—off one and on the other," Johnny Shines wrote in "The Robert Johnson I Knew," a piece included in *The American Folk Music Occasional*. The journal was compiled and edited by Chris Strachwitz and Pete Welding, a jazz critic whose essay, "Hell Hound on His Trail: Robert Johnson," first popularized the Faustian legend. Shines wrote in conclusion, "This was the Robert Johnson that I knew and the good things that I knew about him."

At present, this year of our looking back, we can remember each occasion when the portraits of our lives have been inscribed by our husband's legend. Fifty years ago, Tabitha was offered a choice part in a film for RKO Pictures, *Sidewalks of Brimstone*, whose preliminary prop list included a sign that read, "Nigger, don't let the sun set on you here," a common proclamation found at crossroads throughout the South. The production was shut down owing to budget constraints. Fourteen years ago, Claudette heard a program on NPR debating whether the tree under which Robert Johnson sat when the devil offered his bargain was oak, dogwood, or holly. An anonymous caller verified none of the above. Sixty-two years ago, Betty was told by a friendly but fretful physician that if she kept in her cups she wouldn't last another decade, echoing what the devil was said to have told our husband, "You now got but eight years yet to walk this earth." She celebrated her ninety-third birthday last week. Ten years ago, Mary Sue left a Korean nail salon on York Avenue and 77th Street, her mascara in shambles down each cheek, her fingers only half done with red polish, because she had suddenly remembered the time Robert Johnson corroborated a lie about his nails having been cut at the crossroads 'til they bled. Her wedding band had to be returned by messenger. Still to this day, raising our arms for the security wand at LaGuardia, sitting beneath the dryer at a hair stylist, waiting in line to make another deposit at a local branch, coming just short of exact change at the Winn-Dixie, we are continually reminded of our husband's legacy. What constant have we begun to surmise after this whole time? What perspective have we taken through so much hindsight? Not all legends are saints.

CHAPTER FIVE

The first time he saw The Loblolly, a two-floor hotel located on a gas-lit street in downtown Little Rock, painted a dusty red, crowned in rusty tin, and constructed mainly of its titular pine timber featuring a set of Jalousie windows, Ernie Oertle thought it seemed the kind of place that could keep a secret. Ernie had plenty of secrets. He often traveled to faraway states from his hometown of Jackson, Mississippi, sent on recruiting trips by the ARC label group, a secret he kept from the recruiters for rival labels he often recognized at lunch counters on the road. One of the most reliable talent scouts and salesmen of race records in the mid-South territory, a secret he kept, among others of a more intimate nature, from his mother, Ernie could track down a bluesman and get him under contract before the bluesman even knew Ernie's full name. He kept secrets from his neighbors. He kept secrets from his friends. He kept secrets from his lovers. At the moment, standing in the lobby of an establishment that proclaimed above its door, "White Folk Only," and considering how Arkansas's motto, "The People Rule," just applied to those of a certain color, the most urgent of all Ernie Oertle's secrets was the black musician sitting in the front seat of his automobile.

The black musician was our mutual husband. Earlier in the year, April of 1936, Robert Johnson, twenty-four, had gotten up the will-do to knock on the door of a record shop owned by H.C. Speir, the talent scout who first recorded Son House, Charley Patton, and Skip James. Robert had stood in a line of identical bluesmen with identical aspirations, waited his turn, sat in a room with mattresses nailed to the walls, played his song, and hung around the shop as sides were cut on the premises. Each disc for demo purposes was made of red acetate instead of black vinyl. Afterwards, given the talent scout's apparent lack of enthusiasm for his performance, Robert Johnson left the record shop and continued his travels throughout the South. He was in Little Rock when Ernie Oertle found him. Ernie had been told by his colleague, friend, and mentor H.C. Speir, who'd grown disillusioned with the recording business, that our husband had the goods if only somebody had the gumption.

"And a good evening to you, sir!" Ernie heard someone say on entering the hotel. "Welcome to The Loblolly lobby!"

Across the room, past the deserted sitting area with furniture upholstered in genuine zebra stripe, beneath the mounted head of a lion imprisoned in a silent roar by the taxidermist's art, past the walls lined with photographic evidence of safaris in darker lands, next to a gun rack weighted by six-foot-long rifles with five-inch-wide barrels constructed of heavy red brass, stood one of the most fascinating things Ernie had seen in the whole of his thirty-two years. The desk clerk's name was John William Smith. His dimpled chin was rung with a circle beard, and his dimpled cheeks had known of a straight razor. The lines in his forearms gave him to be of the finest fettle. The pince-nez wedged delicately below his eyebrow appeared more for dramatic effect than correction of sight. The banker's part in his hair emphasized the symmetry in his oval face. Despite the mediocrity of John William Smith's name—he always signed his postcards, most of which we recently sent to the National Handwriting Institute for a complete analysis, with an elaborate nom de plume—Ernie found him to be special proof of God's hand in the order of things.

"I apologize for the 'Loblolly lobby' bit. The owner makes me say it," John William said to Ernie after their formal introductions. "He is partial to the word play. Also, exotic game and foreign hunts."

Ernie said, "I don't say." He went hot in the face. "I mean, *you* don't say."

"But I *do* say. Have you looked at the walls around this place? We've got near to all of Black Africa killed and stuffed and mounted for perusal. It's a zoo in here."

John William had a right gorgeous laugh. Ernie considered it a sound to behold. Those crow's feet on one eye, that hole so deep in his chin.

"You know what? I think I can read your mind, Mr. Oertle. I think I know what you're going to say next. 'Do we have a room available?' Am I close?"

"You're right in quality but not quantity. I was going to ask if you have two rooms available."

"Oh. I mean. Is it, um, is the second room, uh, for your wife? I mean. Well. Perchance."

"Not exactly."

Ernie told John William about "the little problem, the delicate issue" sitting in the front seat of his automobile. He told him how certain Arkansas society might not be tolerant of the situation, that it was simply a fact of nature, that it was the way of the world, why such a dilemma stood as imperative nobody but themselves know. He told him "mummy's the word" and "daddy can't know" with a wink. He told him he only needed a "reasonable solution for this one evening" because in the morning he and "the problem would mosey on their way" to San Antonio. Did John William understand his plight? Bet your fern.

It took half a blink's thought. John William, who in his correspondence to Ernie over the years would sign as Philippe de Rocheport, Aloysius Windingham IV, Peter Piper, Thumbelina, Yankee Doodle, and Xavier Yalo Zatarain, said, "Eureka!" most demurely a man given to extravagance. They brought extent to the matter.

Out of doors, each of them giddy with their plan, John William and Ernie woke our husband by tapping on the dirty windshield. They crossed their index fingers against the lip. They whispered for him to whisper. They motioned that he should follow their lead. What Robert saw, walking over an acre of fenland around ten o'clock at night, could not fill a plumbago, but what Robert heard, approaching the dark outline of a farmhouse with light breaking through its panels, could only be described as clucks.

The chicken coop had a modern design. Constructed with a special U-shape layout bought from Milo Hastings' assistant at the 1915 World's Fair in San Francisco, funded by The Loblolly's rich owner, and chronicled in a 1958 book, *Cow Mangers, Hen Houses, and Bird Cages: The Domestication of America*, by the photographer R.P. Jameson, it provided the chickens with a steady stream of artificial light and housed them in individualized compartments known as laying cages. Such a well-lit, quiet, cozy incubator could offer adequate quarters for anyone looking to spend the night beyond Little Rock's intolerant, watchful eyes.

On first step in the farmhouse, John William said, "You can just, well, hit the hay anywhere," as he surveyed the layer of straw on the ground. Neither Robert nor Ernie accommodated the desk clerk's humor. With a voice near to whisper, he said, "I'll leave you two to say your goodnights," shutting the stall door at his departure.

"Wish we could make some other arrangement," Ernie said to Robert, "but the hotel is very much booked to capacity."

Only two of The Loblobby's fourteen rooms, we know from the hotel register for that night, November 20, 1936, were occupied by other guests, one an Irish ranch hand with knock knees on his way to become a man in El Paso, the other a Mennonite farmer breaking his sacred pact to avoid the Sins of the World.

"Why can't I head over to colored town," Robert said to Ernie, "find myself a room with my own and each?"

"Colored town's too far away."

Standard operating procedure was never to let a Negro under contract near alcohol, firearms, or women, this according to a memo widely circulated around most record labels, for those substances are known to compromise the Negro's ability to uphold its legal obligations to the company.

"I have to admit a truth."

"What's that, Bob?"

"I'm afraid of chickens."

Although we have no proof of this fear—evidence against it would not come to light until early the next morning—we must admit that we do enjoy the irony of his expression. "I'm afraid of chickens." It would seem Ernie Oertle was none the stranger to our own disposition, as he responded to Robert Johnson's statement with a great whoop of laughter. Ernie had been in the business long enough to appreciate Robert's aversion to sleeping in a chicken coop. Bluesmen love to be lonely, but they hate being alone. It doesn't take a play pretty to know that. Near the stall door, his voice mayhap underscored by the steady clatter of an egg rolling down a wobbly chute, Ernie told Robert that they would leave first thing in the morning, rest assured, that they would make San Antonio by the nightfall next. The stammer in Robert's "B-but, p-p-please, d-don't" almost made Ernie to halt. He was all the way out the door, though, before the sentence could finish itself.

The lobby of the hotel testified to quietude on his return. Yet again, putting lions and safaris and rifles to shame, John William waited for him on the other side of the establishment. Smoking a cigarette in the style of the French. Scribbling with a quill pen in a ring-bound ledger. Sipping at a cordial from a Daisy & Button tumbler. Searching his pink tongue for speck of tobacco. Whatever Ernie was thinking at such a moment, be it pleasurable remorse or be it remorseful pleasure, accorded by and by with John William's only question.

"Would you like to see your room?"

The next morning, forehead reflective with fresh sweat and eyes bulbous from lack of sleep, Ernie woke before sunup and crept down the stairs. He found a tin percolator in the kitchen and poured himself a large cup of home roast. He found a candlestick telephone behind the desk and lifted the earpiece from the receiver hook. During those years, phone numbers consisted of two letters and five digits, such as PL-5-3775,

AN-2-4967, and TR-1-3573. The letters were often spoken as words in order to make them more memorable. PL became Plaza, AN became Andrew, TR became Tremont. Although these exchange names usually stayed consistent with their respective areas, Ernie had, most all his life, invented his own names for different phone numbers. Instead of Express-5-3844, the number for his dentist, he would use Excruciate-5-3844. Instead of Fleetwood-2-8934, the number for the bakery, he would use Flour-2-8934. Another exchange name common to Jackson, "Drake," had numerous variations in Ernie's personal system.

"Operator, get me Dread-7-2294." He waited for the connection. "Hello, Mother, it's me."

Susan Hays Oertle, recording secretary of the Junior Auxiliary and supervising den mother of the Cub Scouts, has never accepted our phone calls over the years, but we suspect she always accepted those from her only son, especially the kind made at 5:45 in the morning.

"Mother, I said it's me…On the road…For work. They need Bibles in other towns, too. You know…I have something to tell you…I did the bad thing again…This is the last time, Momma, I swear to God…I'm sorry…I know…I know…I know…No, not that…But it's not bedtime, Momma, it's barely dawn…Okay…Now I lay me down to sleep…I pray the Lord my soul to keep…If I should die before I wake…I pray the Lord my soul to take…Bye-bye, Mother."

Thirty minutes later, after he had retrieved his linen suitcase from the hotel room, after he had tucked a personal check in the hotel ledger, Ernie withstood the morning chill while dashing towards the chicken coop, aroused Robert, got the automobile to crank despite flooding the engine, and escaped The Loblolly. Their ride out of Little Rock was accompanied by passing signage—"Stop at Charley's Pick and Save: Last Fair Deal Gone Down for Twenty Miles" and "The Lord is in Your Heart, The Devil at Your Ear: First Presbyterian Church Next Right"—as well as by complete silence from Robert.

"Were you able to sleep last night?"

Robert nodded.

"Do you want to stop for breakfast?"

Robert shrugged.

Only when Ernie finally decided to bring some noise to the interior, tuning the radio, upping the volume, banging the dashboard, did he glance at Robert and grasp the reason for his silence. In Robert's hand, contrary to Ernie's first thought, was not a piece of straw, and in Robert's mouth, contrary to Ernie's second thought, was not a sore tooth. Our husband was busy using a peg toothpick to dislodge the gristly meat of a chicken from his second and third molars.

On Monday, November 23, 1936, Robert Johnson began the first of only two recording sessions he would make during his short time for this world. The first session lasted three days. Despite *The Blues Almanack*'s claim it was held in KONO, a radio station located atop the Blue Bonnet Hotel, Robert's first session actually took place in San Antonio's Gunter Hotel. A two-room suite had been converted into a makeshift studio. Thick packing blankets were draped along the walls from floor to ceiling, every article of furniture had been removed, and several upright voice boxes were wired into a portable recording system.

More than a few acts were scheduled to record throughout the day. Robert Johnson was third on the roster.

First on the roster was the Chuck Wagon Gang, a western swing band Robert had admired on the wireless some years back, and second on the roster was a Mexican group led by Francisco Montalvo, Andres Berlanga, and Hermanas Barzaza, whose foreign chords struck Robert as a tad messy for wear. Out in the hallway, each act waiting their turn, Robert partook from a growler of mescal left behind by the Mexicans. The worm suited him fine.

"Anything to loose the muse," said Art Slatherley, the ARC recording director, who smoked cigars what made the air hang thick as cotton-bale cloth. "Ain't that right, my boy?"

Robert mumbled yessuh.

"Don't mind him," said Don Law, the artist and repertory supervisor, his white tennis shirt, white pants, white buck shoes, and white watch at contrast with his black hair and olive complexion. "It's your turn, Robert."

"Call me Bob."

A porter trundled somebody's room service down the hall as Robert entered the hotel suite dark with poor wattage. The air smelled thick and sweet like the waiting room of a cathouse, and the carpet looked as damp and warm as the private hair of a fleshpot. Such a place lent itself to sin by analogy. Our husband felt right at home.

On Art Slatherley's get-along-now, Robert set himself up in a corner of the room, positioning a stool in front of the microphone, positioning his ass on top of the stool, and positioning the guitar in front of his chest. He faced into the corner rather than looking out from it. According to the sound engineers and other musicians present, as well as blues historians and other biographers not present, Robert took such an unusual stance either because he was a shy country boy lost in the big city, a claim we know to be entirely false, or because he did not want anybody to steal his licks, something that holds an element of truth, or because he was such the consummate player he knew facing the corner would allow for a deeper, richer element of bass to be heard from the chords and lyrics of his songs. We believe the last one for the most part.

Robert Johnson recorded sixteen sides over the whole three-day session. He wiped his brow twelve times. He broke a string four times. More than once he said, "This one's for my one true love." He took a bathroom break twice in the first session, three times during the second, and once during the third. He dirtied his shirt with vomit twice. Three times he stopped to tune his guitar. Three times he skipped his midday meal. He finished the growler of mescal four times, and the mescal was replenished four times, and he finished the growler of mescal four more times. Five times he whistled instead of singing. Nine times he hummed instead of strumming. He thanked the Lord seven times. He received a certified check for $95 as his advance on the record. He agreed for another session to be held in Dallas eight months later. He dedicated the record to six women.

"Thank you much, my boy," Art Slatherley said on the last day of the session. "We took some good cuts."

"Where's Mr. Law got himself to?"

"Had family matters needed tending."

"Could you tell him something?" Robert said as Art Slatherley led him out of the suite. "I appreciated all he done for the likes."

The hallway was pert near bustling with musicians. Over those first three days of their arrangement at the Gunter Hotel, according to the *San Antonio Light* newspaper as later referenced in the *Encyclopedia of Country Music*, the ARC crew had gotten 105 tracks "under the wire." The number was a record high. So, without any further acknowledgement of Robert still by his side, Art Slatherley stared down the hallway, at bandleaders standing close to mariachi players, at country yodelers milling around trombonists, and said, "Next!"

Thanksgiving was Don Law's least favorite holiday. A British expatriate and Texas newcomer, he disguised his distaste for all things American and Southern by adapting the motley persona of churchgoer, gadfly, cur, man about town, tummler, burgher, puddler, ne'er-do-well, and mensch. He always paid his city and federals. He usually won at contract and auction. He could play the piano in the classical mode, and he could juggle beer bottles six at the time. Don's wife had deserted him without notice shortly after they moved to San Antonio, leaving the forty-year-old as the only caretaker of their son, nineteen, daughter, eight, and finch, three-quarters. Although Don Jr., a freshman at Princeton, blamed his father for his mother's absence, Rebecca, a gold-star student in second grade, worshiped the man she woke every morning by provoking the neighbor's golden retriever to lick his face alert.

It was for these reasons Don Law could barely finish his hors d'oeuvre. At Pierre & Louis & Philippe, the only French restaurant in all Bexar County, Don sat across from Marilee

Watson, his lady friend of the past four weeks. Tomorrow was Thanksgiving. He had left Rebecca, who yesterday gave her father a turkey made of brown construction paper studded with popcorn, under the care of the teenager from next door, Annabel Cunningham, a 4-H All-Star said to be a good influence on younger girls. Don Jr. had decided not to come home from college for the holidays. The thought of Don's little girl at home without family on the night before Thanksgiving sent the A&R man's usually seaworthy digestive system into a fit of reflux, contraction, and nausea.

"How is your *foie gras*?" Marilee asked Don. "My *foie gras* is delicious."

"The proper way to pronounce it is *foie gras*, dear." How could he ever receive a woman who uttered, not once but twice, the ridiculous phrase of 'phooey grass?' "It's not the best I've had, but this is south Texas."

"Mine is delicious."

Don sipped at his water and considered the wine list. The trick of the evening would be to choose a vintage palatable to himself as well as to his companion. Marilee was two years older than Don, so the wine must be on the younger side. She kept books for the county school system, so it should be a red with good structure. She had never once left the country on a trip, so it should be the product of a foreign vineyard. Marilee was also a grass widow with little savings, so the wine had to be reasonably inexpensive. Don motioned for the waiter and said, "Romanée Saint Vivant, 1934," a Burgundy from Noellat that cost $4.25 before the sommelier surcharge. The waiter complimented his choice. At the same moment, another waiter arrived at the table and placed a black telephone in front of

Don, the extension wire snaking around the other tables all the way back to the kitchen. Of course it was Art Slatherley.

"Donny boy. I hoped I'd catch you there. Listen to me now. We have an issue just come about with our new boy. He got picked up downtown on a vagrancy charge. Here's what I need from you. Go to the station—it's right around the corner, won't take but a minute—and post bail. This is *your* problem. Got that? This ain't *my* problem. I think you know the kind of money this boy can make for the company. Still besides, he took a shine to you during the sessions. All right then. I'll give you a ring tomorrow morning once you've taken care of it all. Good things. Enjoy your frog food."

Art could talk faster than any Southerner Don had met since his arrival stateside. After he explained the situation to Marilee, telling her there was no reason to cancel dinner, letting her know he would be back in five minutes, Don left Pierre & Louis & Philippe and ran down Market Street to St. Mary, scuffing the white suede of his bucks as he mounted the steps of the Police & Fire Building. The officer on duty had been advised of the matter. On word of the official report, Robert Johnson had been picked up for vagrancy, not an uncommon charge throughout the city proper, but the report also stated the site of his arrest, 405 W. 12th St., which happened to be the address of Robert's hotel. Don chose not to pursue the issue any much further. He compensated the fine of twenty dollars, endorsed the blotter, and situated himself in the booking room.

"Thank the Lord up above," Robert said as the officer brought him out of the holding block. "And thank you, too, Mr. Law."

The police officer told him not to mention it.

"I think he was talking to me," Don said. He escorted Robert to the street. "I want you to do as I say, Bob, alright now?"

"Yes, sir."

"Go straight back to your hotel. Don't make any stops this time of night, or the beat cops will pick you up again. Here's forty-five cents. Should be plenty to buy a hot meal. Buy yourself a hot meal. Understood? You need to eat a hot meal."

At Robert's affirmation, Don turned away without saying goodbye and headed back to the restaurant, where he found Marilee fingering the tongs of a salad fork. Her fine crystal glass stood empty on the white damask cloth. The wine was half gone. Forty-five minutes later, more than enough time for Marilee to settle the matter with Don by consuming another bottle, the two of them were just finishing their dinners, he the *pot au feu*, she the *coq au vin*, when a waiter once again placed the black telephone in front of Don. This time it was our husband. His was the first agreeable voice Don had heard in almost an hour. His was also the first sober voice Don had heard in almost an hour.

"I'm sorry to disturb your nice meal, sir, but Mr. Slatherley said you'd be able to aid in my predicament."

"No bother at all, Bob." It was a bit hard for Don to hear over the hiccoughs from his dinner companion. "Really. How can I help?"

The content of their talk remains in dispute amongst us today. According to the legend, first introduced by Don Law and later propagated by Johnny Shines, Robert Johnson said over the telephone, "I'm lonesome." Don asked why. "I'm lonesome and there's a lady here," Robert said. "There's a lady here and she's a kindly one." Don asked what. "The lady wants fifty cents," Robert said, "but I lacks me a nickel."

Only a few of us believe in such a tale. During the first decade of her career, Tabitha, the movie star, was offered a more opportunistic version of "fifty cents" by lecherous studio heads enough times to justify her belief in the story. During the last decade of her career, Helena, the activist, watched too many of her fellow radicals eventually become "kindly ones" of the corporate world for her to permit any doubt in the story. The rest of us do not blame them, but we stand firm in our resolve. Robert always kept a spare dime inside the liner of his hat.

"I don't want to go pick up some musician downtown," Marilee said. "I haven't even finished my cuckoo van."

Despite our disagreement concerning the phone call, we are of the same mind in terms of the events to follow. Don waved for the check. He scripted his name under the tab slot and printed his account number beside the total. The carbon now resides in our dossier. Within fifteen minutes, not including the time it took Marilee to comprehend the W.C. as the proper whereabouts for her toilet, Don drove to San Antonio's colored neighborhood on the east side, China Grove, found the midnight-ramble house where he'd told Robert to wait, Miss Tinkerton's Palace of Crimson Light, gave a nod to the bouncer, David Crockett Myers, and let the engine idle until Robert was brought to the corner, Whippoorwill at Triple Pines.

"You're staying at my house tonight, Bob. Not going to have one of my artists at some two-bit litter box."

Marilee, who'd fallen asleep during the meanwhile, gave nary a thought to the new passenger, being as she was, after all, unconscious the whole trip. Don gently shook her awake when they reached her apartment. He didn't even walk her to the front door, poor woman, but she kept good and steady on her feet. At the Law residence, a Victorian two-story in Southtown, our husband was shown hospitality in kind—a tour of the premises and an offer for coffee and a hand with his bag—certainly not Robert's first occasion to rest his soulless self within the good lives of good people. Don asked the houseguest to see to his daughter as Don himself saw to the babysitter. It was already past Rebecca's bedtime, but he could let her stay up a bit longer.

On his return from walking Annabel across the street to her house, Don hurried frantically into his living room after hearing someone he thought to be an intruder. What he found there was nothing but child's play. Robert and Rebecca sat on the floor facing each other, Indian-style, their hands held up in front of their faces, alternately touching the thumb of one hand with the index of the other. Both of them were singing a nursery rhyme. "The inky winky spider went up the water spout. Down came the rain and washed the spider out—" they waggled their fingers at each other "—Out came the sun and dried up all the rain. And the inky winky spider went up the spout again." Don had never heard Robert sing with such melodic clarity. He sounded like a different person from the person who sang at the recording sessions, but Robert's voice was not the voice of the intruder Don had heard on first entering the house.

"Time for bed, sweetie."

"Five more minutes! Uncle Robert promised to teach me one more song. Please, please?"

"Now you. Just one more."

Don went into the kitchen to pour himself a nightcap. The

eighteen-year-old Scotch reminded him of his own history. Rebecca had always taken after her mother. Both of them liked mayonnaise on their eggs. Both of them cracked their toe knuckles as a habit. Both of them refused to wear gloves in winter. One had dark brown hair, the other bright yellow. One tried to mimic his gait on their evening walks about town. The other had written a pink "goodbye" in lipstick across the vanity. At those memories, standing in earshot of our husband teaching his daughter a nursery rhyme, Don Law closed his eyelids all the sudden heavy with exhaustion, forgot about the double image of a word's reflection coming from the mirror, and listened to the curious sound, that loss of a lilt, that gain of depth, of a little girl becoming a woman.

Erskine Crawford lost himself in blaming his wife for the breakdown. The series of oversights he had made throughout the past few weeks—visiting with his friend at the filling station rather than checking under the hood of his car, whistling cakewalk music instead of listening for the whir of a fan belt on threads—did not occur to him while standing in a ditch along Route 9. Erskine could only think of Mildred. Although they'd spent eleven years of marriage without so much as spilt salt for argument, he would later tell us at a rest home for single seniors in East Texas, Erskine faulted his wife on that hot day in July, as thick steam rose straight up from his radiator grill, simply because she had told him that morning, "Drive careful, honey sweet, drive careful."

He was coated in Wakefield oil up to the elbow. Erskine had never been much with his hands, at least when it came to things mechanical. Around the time of his youth, he had been pretty good with animals, noodling shotten catfish from underwater logs with his bare hands, splinting the wings of fallen quail with a homemade plaster. That particular aspect of his nature might could have been the reason that Erskine suddenly found himself surrounded by what was probably hundreds but what seemed more like thousands of wild jackrabbits.

They came in droves from the grassy field extending up against the ditch, all hopping in the same direction but many stopping to nibble at foodstuff, anything from clumps of daisies to Erskine's very own brogues. He had never seen an incident along such lines. All of the jackrabbits constituted a heather, cream, and russet phalanx of fur moving from one side of the field, over the car, around the car, under the car, and into the other side of the field. Just as sudden as they'd come to appear, though, the jackrabbits vanished into the nettles on the side yonder, leaving nothing but a crackle of dry grass and tiny brown dots of shit. Only one jackrabbit was left behind, pretty standard account, except it was the size of a man.

Rather, initially and briefly and explicably, Erskine mistook the man for a jackrabbit. He was walking west along Route 9 with the sun behind his back. A long bar of black extended in silhouette from the man's neck. Considered in tandem with the man's head, the long, black bar appeared to be a set of giant rabbit ears, but on Erskine's closer inspection, he realized it was just the neck of a guitar slung across the man's back.

All Erskine could think to say was the question, "Did you see those damn rabbits!" What else really, given the situation, was there to ask?

"What rabbits?"

Erskine reached for a hip flask of Irish import in the chevron pocket of his shirt, but all he found was a rag slick with grease from the brokedown fan belt. How could this stranger not have seen a thousand jackrabbits crossing the road? Erskine did not think he had the look of a soft-brain. Gospel truth, the stranger appeared such the observant, keen, confident, wily type as to put everybody around him in a condition of nerves. The look of this man could return any man to childhood. Erskine was so much taken with gooseflesh that he was just barely able to squeak, "You didn't see the bunnies?"

"No, sir. I did not see the bunnies," the stranger said, resetting his trilby. "Might I ask you for a ride? That is, sir, if you're going towards Dallas."

At such polite phrasing of the query, as he would tell us while standing before a mantle without any family photos, as he would tell us again while sitting at a table with a place setting for one, Erskine calmed like a baby at the teat. Good manners certainly go a long way among the black folk of Texas.

"Sure, you can have a ride," Erskine said, cupping his hand as he got a cigarette on its feet, "but only if you can part with that cowhide round your waist."

It took Erskine Crawford no time at all to fasten Robert Johnson's belt as a substitute for his engine's fan belt. He lowered the hood and swabbed his forehead. He coiled the bucket springs and gripped the steering wheel. He turned the ignition and giddyapped the engine. On hearing their efforts catch, Robert, still standing by the front fender, picked up his duffel bag and walked to the passenger door, each step erasing the jigsaw of paw prints on the ground. They were a mile down the road before either of them made for talk.

Erskine asked the stranger, "Why you heading to Dallas?" as they passed a sign reading ten miles to the city limits.

"To get more famous."

"Man who speaks in the comparative must already have a stake in the matter." Erksine, who had not only graduated with high marks in rhetoric and composition from Howard University, but who had also gotten misty in the eye on first reading the picture book *Raggedy Ann Stories*, took note of the young man's perplexity. "What I mean to ask is are you already taken for famous?"

"I'm Robert Johnson," the stranger said. "The famous bluesman."

"Robert Johnson, it's nice to meet you. How about that? Robert Johnson, the famous bluesman."

Over the next few minutes, our husband gave Erskine a full account of his newfound success in the recording industry. All of us have heard the same story well enough. During the six months following his first recording session, Robert had cut trails all throughout the state of Mississippi, making quick sojourns home so he could tell each family of his singular triumph. Claudette, the archivist, still owns the original 78 he carried under his arm as he walked up the dirt road to their house, the record's dark shellac disc, off-center spindle hole, and thin paper sleeve now cased within a walnut frame and real glass, its labels of "Not Licensed for Radio Broadcast" and "Vocal Blues with Guitar Acc." overlooking a desk cluttered with company notepads, Troll Dolls, and gelatin stress relievers. Betty, the drunk, has mostly forgotten the day he knocked on her door wearing a piano scarf, cap-toe leather oxfords, and a boater hat, all of which he had bought with royalties from the

American Record Corporation and most of which she later traded for a case of decent Canadian rye. Although the question never occurred to us at the time, we often ask ourselves, so many years from those few months, *Who did he tell first?*

"Soon to be the best bluesman in the whole wide world?" Erskine was looking at our husband with a remarkable lack of condescension. "Well then, Robert, my congratulations to you and yourn."

A cattle gate along the road caused the car to stall for a frightful second, such that Robert's "thank you much" got lost in the commotion. It took a minute for them to shift back up to the speed limit of thirty miles per hour.

"Do you mind if I ask after your people?" Erskine said, not yet aware of the cancer devouring his own wife's breast. "Is there a Missus Johnson?"

Robert's voice fell to the octave of confession. "I'd be lying if I told you there wasn't one, and my momma didn't raise me to be no liar."

"I'm sure you're a good man to her."

"The love of a woman is a funny business," Robert said, a touch of revelry stenciling the corners of his eyes. "Makes your heart feel drunk."

"True as told."

Out the window, where the neighborhoods of Dallas were slipping past like a reel for *The March of Time* at the picture show, a group of women mingled on flagstone sidewalks in their Sunday finery, a group of men loaded their meerschaum pipes near the church, and a group of children flipped jacks on break from Bible school. The busy city knew from a day of rest. Erskine tried his hardest, clenching his jaw and shutting his lips, to pretend the moisture claiming a path down his cheek, cold against his jaw and wet along his lips, was only a stray bit of sweat. He drove careful.

"You can drop me off right here on the corner."

At Harwood and Bryan, a cross section on the north side of downtown, Erskine, slightly riled that our husband did not address him as sir, pulled to the curb and shifted to neutral. He wasn't upset for long. "That young man was getting out the cab when up comes this big gust of wind, *whoosh*, and blows the hat off his head," Erskine would tell his wife over dinner that night. "So the last I saw of that poor boy was of his ass zigging and zagging down Harwood, chasing after that damn hat."

Mildred put her best face towards her husband's story, even though she was in the worst part of another of her spells. She had hardly touched her food. While Erskine kept on about his afternoon with the country boy—he was known locally for regular attempts to do good by black folk who hadn't gotten the same advantages as him—Mildred picked up both of their dinner plates, the green beans solidifying in the bacon drippings, the cornbread falling to pieces, the slices of ham blanching under a glaze of redeye, and carried them to the kitchen sink. "So I leaned out the window and hollered at him," Erskine said on her return to the table, "I yelled, 'Good luck to you, son, because you sure are going to need it!'" He laughed at the memory, and he looked at his wife. He said that he loved her, and he said that he loved her. Mildred could barely hear him through the pain. Despite the tremors overtaking her hands, she summoned enough strength to pour her husband a second cup of coffee, meant to aid his poor digestion. She did not spill a drop.

⁂

In the downtown business district of Dallas, Texas, starting Saturday, June 19, 1937, and ending Sunday, June 20, 1937, the second and final recording session of Robert Johnson's career took place above a Buick showroom. The producers had chosen a weekend for the session because of a heat wave choking the city of late. They'd also hoped the weekend would be more apt for quiet. On the first day of recording, however, the din of street traffic below the upstairs level of the showroom, horn wail and tire tread and brake pitch, overwhelmed the studio space already filled with spare horns, spare tires, and spare brakes, each part featuring the tri-shield Buick family crest.

"To keep the street noises out, we had to keep the windows closed," Don Law would later say of the session, "so we worked shirtless with electric fans blowing across cakes of ice."

The scene must have made for a sight. On one side of the room stood the crew from Brunswick Records, including two producers, Don Law and Art Slatherley, and a recording engineer, Vince Liebler. Their heads were combed heavy with Brylcreem. On the other side of the room sat the Crystal City Ramblers, four old-time bluegrass players from Arlington County, Virginia. Their beards were Dutch in length. In the middle of the room stood five stockmen with thick burnsides, Zeke Williams and His Rambling Cowboys, each busy splattering the floor with ambeer while talking to Robert Johnson. His modest hit, "Terraplane Blues," had impressed them. Everyone was as naked as the first time they'd made their mothers cry, except of course for their boxer shorts and the occasional calf garter. We can picture it just now.

Although Robert's initial recording session had been regarded as the work of a professional, inventive but adequate, skillful but derivative, this second session would establish his place within the history of blues music. He approached the mike. He sat on the stool. He positioned his guitar. The hubris of one Casey taking his time at the plate, the discipline of another driving his train full-steam: Our husband sure was at himself. Robert flexed his long fingers as he had once seen of Leroy Carr, whose haint supposedly visits bluesmen whenever their knuckles fail to crack. Robert winked for the engineer to flip the switch like he'd been told Bumble Bee Slim, Peetie Wheatstraw, and Peg Leg Howell were wont to do in their own sessions from way back. Robert loosened his spine and curved his shoulders in the manner of Blind Lemon Jefferson and Blind Willie McTell, both of whom some say could buckshot a pigeon on a telegraph line at 400 yards.

Overall, Robert Johnson made thirteen masters during the two days of recording, three on the first and ten on the second. Eleven would be released within the next year. "Stones in My Passway," "I'm a Steady Rollin' Man," and "From Four Till Late." "Hellhound on My Trail" and "Little Queen of Spades." "Malted Milk" and "Drunken Hearted Man." "Me and the Devil Blues," "Stop Breakin' Down Blues," and "Traveling Riverside Blues." "Love in Vain." "Honeymoon Blues" and "Milkcow's Calf Blues." Although twelve alternate takes were made in total from each session, not to mention the rumors of another original song, The Lost Track, supposedly made around a year before his death, the final number of songs our husband recorded during his lifetime would never exceed the number twenty-nine.

Everybody around the showroom was put into a genuine state of flabbergast. Art Slatherley was appreciative. Vince Liebler was distraught. Don Law was congratulatory. What about the Crystal City Ramblers and Zeke Williams and His Rambling Cowboys? The jealousy from each of those musical acts went beyond their respective capacity for verbal articulation. Naught but one thing could be taken into account of the session. Melodies of such skillful innovation had no cognate in the musical canon of Dixie.

"He was doing some of everything you heard. If you liked it, you did it. So, no doubt, you go in the studio to record it," Johnny Shines would later say of his friend boy's influences. "He just do the stuff that comes to his mind, for instance, because he had no set plan for no recording session."

At last flash of the stoplight, Art and Don approached Robert with their hands out in front so to shake his own. Both of the men told him he had a bright future ahead of him. They said he would be rich and they said he would be famous. Don asked whether he would be available for another session next fall. Art asked whether a five-percent royalty was fine with him. Robert said yes to both. About Art's question, the one concerning the percentage of his royalties, our husband was right. Not even white musicians got five points on the barrelhead. About Don's question, the one concerning his availability next fall, our husband was wrong.

What Vince "Rutabaga" Liebler needed to do most of all, more than drag on a hand-roll of Bull Durham, more than gulp at a half-quart of Shiner Bock, was spend a good ten minutes in the men's bathroom. The red marks of fingernails covered the white insides of his forearm. Since the start of recording earlier in the day, over hours of song after song and take after take from our husband, Rutabaga hadn't been able to get away in order to see a man about a dog. Don Law kept asking for just one more cut, and Art Slatherley kept saying just five more minutes. The Sunday session finally ended at six o'clock on Sunday night.

Rutabaga closed the bathroom door behind him. He unzipped his kit and he rolled his sleeve. He struck a match. He pulled the plunger. He found a vein. He tied the strap and he gnashed his teeth. Mind this was only but 1937. Rutabaga was on the needle years before America felt a prick.

Outside the Buick showroom, standing on the sidewalk, Rutabaga took a long breath of evening air and felt wholly at peace with himself. Isn't it remarkable the variations on Tai Chi and other techniques of relaxation that men pick up when they spend their twenties stationed on a Navy base in the Philippines? Across the street, Robert Johnson was sitting on the curb, guitar case between his knees, sign for the local behind his back. Rutabaga cupped his mouth to amplify the holler.

"Need a ride?"

It took Rutabaga near about five minutes to convince Robert he certainly wasn't "some hitch in his get-along" before Robert lastly gave to join Rutabaga for a drive. On their way uptown, Dallas's three chief materials of construction, grey cinder blocks and grey asphalt and grey pavement slabs, set the background as the two men, one black and one white, rode side by side in a convertible cabriolet. Robert did warm to Rutabaga. They talked at how Robert had been given four bits traveling money so he could take the train home, that he would probably have to spend the night at some flophouse because trains out of town probably wouldn't be running on a weekend night, why Robert didn't have one but six possible train destinations that he occasionally called home, that having to choose any of them over the others wrought so much vexation he almost didn't want to choose at all. Neither man gave it a sigh for comment.

"Why don't you stay with me tonight?" Rutabaga said. "I got a spare room back of the house."

"No, sir. I couldn't."

"We'd go out on the town for good measure. There's a roadhouse outside of city limits always gets cooking on the Sabbath. All night long women are dropping their drawers. The big-legged kind. Come morning customers even get breakfast on the house. Eggs, hot biscuits, grits, bacon."

Our husband never could turn down an offer of hot biscuits.

"You're going to love the place. Sunday night party full of a Saturday night crowd. Music thick as the whiskey, whiskey sweet as the music. Texas place of business with a Mississippi kind of sound. We'll head over soon as we drop your bag at my house."

"Hell with my bag," Robert said. "Let's go right now."

"We got to pick somebody up first."

The Texas sky had gone from pink to purple to pitch by the time they got Rutabaga's sister in the rumble seat. At twenty-five years old, Vivian Liebler was younger than her brother by eighteen years. She put Robert in a state. Her shirtwaist uniform from the stapler factory showed streaks of machine oil at its sailor collar. Her bobtail of yellow hair encased in a snood dangled a ruby brooch decorated with the blue matte of a teakettle. Vivian was delicate and arrogant and impudent and beautiful, a hothouse flower of a woman. She was form in want of essence, no how the type for a bluesman.

"Nice to meet you, miss. My name's Robert."

"Pleasure. Vivian."

"Be kind to the man, sissy. He's my friend."

Despite each and every of his iniquities present and past though not future, Rutabaga, partial to labeling himself a progressive, celebrated the African race through the glory of their varying degrees of Negritude. The provenance of such a disposition lay within the vicinity of his religious creed. Rutabaga Liebler was an Automat Christian. He chose what he wanted from faith and he paid for what he got in change. Down his spine he had a tattoo that read, "Do Unto Others," an ellipsis breadcrumbing into his tailbone, though he'd been too drunk to remember getting the ink. He enjoyed a good fight. He prayed each morning. He slept with plenty of women. He did not attend church. On the day he'd baptized himself in a flood canal, the two-foot-deep water carried a flotsam that included supermarket circulars and lambskin prophylactics, the latter of which belonged to him.

Those were the reasons why Rutabaga worried for his younger sibling. She was neither Christian nor progressive. Ever since their parents died, leaving Vivian in his charge, Rutabaga had done his mightiest to educate his sister, such to the extent that she'd become a genuine fan of the blues and its makings, what from late nights to swoop whiskey to juke joints. Still, there was no rightful telling how she would react to a Negro sitting close enough for his breath to graze her virginal, pale cheek.

"Hope you don't mind, Vivian. Thought we'd stop by for a listen," Rutabaga said as they pulled into a parking lot aforetime built for livery carriages. "Robert, take a look at the place. Did I tell you? Tell me did I tell you."

Originally founded as a stable for lease to cotton growers, Monkey Shines, currently incarnated for the purposes of showcasing race music from parts all over, yielded body and breeches to contradiction. Ruckus juice for sale was distilled in a milk barn out back. Salad bowls served for ashtrays, drum barrels served for dance stands, salt shakers served for shot glasses. Picnic tablecloth was draped as curtains over the front windows. Home to all manner of badman from about the region, including sneak thieves and street buskers, road agents and highwaymen, lintheads, knuckledusters, and ruffians, Monkey Shines was commonly frequented by gentlemen seeking respite from their fortunate upbring. We are certain their families thought they really were at the country club. Wives and children will believe just about anything.

Robert made tracks straight to the bar. He was following directly behind Vivian, who did not want him in tow, Rutabaga could just tell by her look. He had other things on his mind. It did not take any time at all for Rutabaga to become enthralled by the sound of a woman singing the blues on the stage across the room. He did not notice the men playing eight ball, his game, on a pool table fashioned from a card table, nor did he pay any mind to the waitress carrying pink gin, his drink, in glasses ordinarily used for preserving jam. Rutabaga could only register the blues woman. Her body suited him down to the ground. Her face curled his liver on sight. She no doubt appeared to be comeatable.

At the end of "Memphis Blues," the woman, later to identify herself as Lucille Masterson, stepped from the stage and loitered beneath a sign that read, "No Lottering." Damned if she wasn't staring right back at Rutabaga. He walked to her and nodded his greetings. She nodded back. Her mouth said, "Hi," but her eyes said, "Hello there."

"I certainly did enjoy your set," Rutabaga told the woman, "though I only caught the tail end of it."

"My tail end is the best part."

Over his few years in the industry, Rutabaga had known plenty of lady bluesmen by their records, including Mamie Smith, "First Lady of the Blues," as well as Ma Rainey, "Mother of the Blues," but he had never come across a lady bluesman live in the flesh. Disappointment this Sunday evening was as likely as a clean shirt in a dogfight, Rutabaga knew by what he had learned so far of this Lucille Masterson. Something in her throat sounded to feel like smooth pebbles, and something in her color looked to taste of sorghum syrup. Rutabaga took a fancy to her sensibility. He had been with his fair share of the opposite sex, but he had never had a decent stake in the opposite race.

"What do you call your name?"

"My mother called it Vince. Others call it Rutabaga."

"Why?"

"Never bothered to ask."

The 1937 diary for Vince Rutabaga Liebler contains entries for every single day of the year. On Sunday, June 20, an entry titled "The Worst Night of My Life" in walnut ink, Rutabaga describes Lucille Masterson as "the most beautifull, intamate, and forwerd woman I've thought to have known in alls my life." He tells of how he courted her. "Never understood how some Christians could believe dancing be for the devil. Not so for me! Not so for her! We got sweaty on each others." At halfway through the entry, just before the unthinkable was to occur, Rutabaga writes, "Lucille asked me to take her to one of the rooms upstairs and I have never been so happy in all my whole life."

Rutabaga glanced over at the bar to check on Vivian and Robert, but all he could see was a Chinese with eyes like a sideyard gidge. No matter. They must have parted ways by now. They must be somewhere in the crowd. On his way to Monkey Shines' second floor, where rooms were kept explicitly for the purposes of doing sex, Rutabaga made talk with Lucille in attempt to distract one of them, he wasn't sure which, from mentioning the obvious matter.

"I truly admire that song you sang, 'The Memphis Blues,'" Rutabaga said. "First heard it myself on Beale Avenue years ago."

"Ain't you mean Beale *Street*?"

"Not in my day."

His concern in this situation, one thing Rutabaga probably should but actually didn't want to know, was whether he'd be charged. Lucille never had a chance to speak of it. The two of them fell into Room Five going at it in a haphazard way. They tangled their arms. Each of their mouths stuck to its counterpart. They wrangled their legs. Instead of doing what should have come natural, choosing the bed for their relations, Rutabaga kicked away the Queen Anne chair and pushed Lucille up against the Governor Winthrop dresser. She tasted and felt and smelt and looked exactly as he had expected when he first heard her on stage. Rutabaga slid his hand up the creamy down landscape of her inner thigh, just like a man, getting his pointer finger ready to check the oil and ring the bell.

Lucille's member hung about yay long. It was held in place between cheeks and behind undergarment by rigging of an intricate sort. There was twine where there should have been lace. There was tape where there should have been frill. Rutabaga drew his mouth from that of Lucille Masterson, formerly one Louis Desclavage of unknown heritage, with the kind of horror that renders dramaturgy impotent. His silent face had the sculpture of a howl. Nothing of a piece in this whole world, like as not, could be worse than a piece on this woman. Rutabaga thought himself a fool and a sinner. He felt he should reclaim his manhood with a rally of fisticuffs, but all he could muster was putting heel to toe out the room.

"The dog's foot! You know you knew the whole time," Lucille said as Rutabaga closed the door behind him. "Smart man like you always know what's at stake. The goose honks high!"

On his way through Monkey Shines, considering himself a coward, Rutabaga staggered past local gentry with sweat playing tectonics on their linen suits, a Seeburg in the corner rendering a ballad called "President McKinley," and matronly servers bearing in each hand platters of goody bread. It had to be later than he'd thought if the house breakfast was already begun. Rutabaga couldn't find any sight of his sister and friend, what with the little effort he gave the matter, because his mind was preoccupied by a more urgent concern. Could you catch Cupid's Itch via the mouth? He did not want to think of the whereabouts those lips had made for a siphon. God knew. Rutabaga pulled from his back pocket the miniature edition of a Bible he'd been given by his minister, Harold Clopton, though he much rather needed the last of what he'd bought the other week from his launderer, Mr. Yin.

His medical kit was in the glovebox. Outside of Monkey Shines, the cool air relieving his hot collar, the dark night soothing his light head, Rutabaga wove his way through the parking lot, still full this time of night, until he caught glimpse of his cabriolet. Moonglade swathed its hood in the palest of color. Rutabaga couldn't remember raising the convertible top, but then again, his thoughts were reeling in fourteen languages. He fetched up all standing. Rutabaga saw the bare hindquarters of our husband rising and falling in the whitleather rumble seat. Rutabaga heard the husky moan of his sister begging loud and hard from the matrimonial position. Although for many years we never knew about this event, we can each and all testify to one eternal truth in the nature of man. Jagged ice will always get a drink the coldest.

Rutabaga pulled Robert Johnson from the car and tossed him into the gravelly dirt. He told Vivian to stay put and keep her damn mouth shut. He lost his Bible for a moment but saw it near his feet. Rutabaga kicked Robert Johnson in his naked crotch and stomped him in the flat of his stomach. That was right when he really started in on him. Despite Rutabaga's honest provocation—each of us angrily understands his incomprehensible rage—we find it excruciating to imagine the pain our husband endured. He was a fiend in love, but he was our fiend. We prefer to think of the Bible that had fallen in the dirt. Perhaps, as Robert was beaten to within a foot of his life, those soft covers lay open on the ground of the parking lot. Perhaps, as another woman screamed for mercy on him, those thin pages were flipped by wind to the passage Mark 5:9. "Our name is Legion," it reads, "for we are many."

"Walkin' Blues"

Although our husband's death remains the greatest mystery of his life—who did it, where did it happen, why do it, when did it happen—the event has given rise over the years to dozens of other mysteries, each of which has come to be considered a practice run for the challenge of its forebear. Historians usually dropped their lines of investigation after arriving at what they deemed a loose end. We took up the slack. Journalists often quit digging through layers of research after they turned up nothing but worthless information. Our taps lay closer to the source. Throughout the decades since Robert Johnson's departure from this world, all of us, unaided by the other, unknown to the other, unwanted by the other, have managed to resurrect parts of him in our lives by scrambling, each at different times, each at different places, to find answers to the questions he left behind.

It is widely accepted that Robert Johnson recorded only twenty-nine songs during his lifetime. A small faction of blues enthusiasts and their fanatical ilk, however, believe in the existence of an additional song. Many have searched for the lost track, but few have been near to finding it.

Helena led the pursuit. In the autumn of 1988, following years of little success, the activist of our group came closest to making the discovery. She realized that Canada was the most likely home of the thirtieth song after tracing the route

Robert Johnson once took while traveling the country. From June of 1937 to May of 1938, he had walked the blues with his friend Johnny Shines, playing their music to audiences hungry for a new sound. Yankees had never heard the likes of it. Several stops along his circuit were cities in the province of Nova Scotia. Helena drove to Halifax in her current husband's '83 Toyota Mark II, its backseat covered in blank gridlines for crossword puzzles, its trunk filled with the amateur reporter's panoply of equipment: typewriter, spyglass, flashlight, tweezers, fake nose, fake glasses, fake hair, carton of legal pads, box of golf pencils, tape recorder, and microphone. She also planned to use a New England accent for effect. Helena's preference in motion pictures was exclusive to the work of Katherine Hepburn.

The people of Canada were hot and cold in the figurative sense. Almost everyone Helena spoke with expressed a fondness for the blues, but none could recall anything of Robert Johnson coming through their parts. A few people chose not to converse much at all. They leered at Helena, the men gumming tobacco cud and the women darning pot holders, as if to drawl, "We do not take kindly to strangers," except in our heads the phrase assumed a shrill Canuck twang. It also included the coda, "Don't y'know, yah?"

Helena took Marine Drive from Halifax, passing through coastal villages along the way, including Murphy's Cove, Smith Settlement, Dartmouth, Mushaboom, Tangier, Oyster Ponds, and Fern Hill. Most of them didn't warrant a deep study. Fishmongers and lobstermen worried at the stains of their trade, the sweat marks, the fish goop, as Helena questioned them about old stories of an enigmatic musician. She still had the attributes of a looker even in her eighties. Dockworkers and ferrymen decried their poor conditions for labor, the long hours, the low wages, as Helena nodded her head in sympathetic but taciturn agreement. She still had the bearing of a socialist even in the eighties. At the Seaforth Grill, a roadside shanty with a chalkboard menu, she received her first and only positive response to questions concerning Robert Johnson. The man was known as Daffy. Octogenarian, retired sea captain, and teetotaler, "Daffy" was so nicknamed not because he was crazy, according to a waitress, but because he was "flipping Looney Tunes."

"I remember a colored fellow coming through here in the late thirties. Had a guitar. He played like an angel," Daffy said to Helena, ratcheting her pulse. "But he was actually an alien. He took me aboard his spacecraft. Flew like a dream."

On her drive home, Helena left the car's windows down, letting gridlines escape the back seat. Her husband would be mad at her for leaving without word. Helena didn't care anymore. She watched the paper twirl and twist in the cold wind through the rearview mirror. She stared at the black and white sheets scattering in the snow banks along the wet highway. All Helena could think was the question, *What's a seven-letter word for "unsuccessful venture"?* Failure and divorce fit just about perfect.

Claudette endured problems of her own when seeking the details surrounding the death of our husband's first child. Her life as the archivist of our group was mainly a solitary one. Perhaps that, her loneliness, was why Claudette became so obsessed with discovering the name of the child, a boy, who died along with his mother, our predecessor, during the painful birth. We knew the exact date of his death. We knew the exact reasons for his death. We even knew that his little body was cremated and scattered by our husband across his father-in-law's land. What we did not know was the word our predecessor had traced in her own blood when our husband found her on the floor of their house. Robert would only divulge its number of letters. It is unbelievable how many names have six characters to them.

Despite years and years of effort, tracking relatives of the mother, interviewing the doctor, interviewing the nurse, pondering letters from the father, Claudette was never able to solve the mystery. She might as well have tried to unearth the bullet-riddled body of Mr. James Hoffa. She might as well have tried to surface the coral-encrusted remains of Ms. Amelia Earhart. Let us not forget the reason we have no physical proof of Sasquatch, the Yeti, or Bigfoot is their race most likely buries its dead. Claudette has never forgiven herself. To this day, the manila folder titled, "Child, First," a subsection of the file, "Family," within the cabinet labeled, "Wife, First," remains empty.

Tabitha filled a brief lull between film projects for Warner Bros. and United Artists by searching for the last stanza to our husband's best work. Although Ike Zinnerman had been interrupted before he could finish "Preaching Blues," years later recorded by Robert Johnson as an homage to his mentor, the full lyrics of the song were rumored to exist scrawled on a throwaway scrap of paper, something along the lines of a cigarette pack empty but for leftover flakes, a matchbook, a business card, a napkin, or a receipt for groceries bought on somebody else's charge account. It was in the summer of 1964 that Tabitha set out on her mission.

On his death, Ike Zinnerman's few possessions had made

a pilgrimage across the country, from his sister in Toledo to his cousin in Scranton, from his uncle in Miami to his other uncle in Chicago, from his niece in Santa Fe to his nephew in Minneapolis. They had finally ended up in Biloxi, Mississippi, of all places, less than twenty miles from where Tabitha was born. The plane trip consisted of three layovers. Tabitha had to take a bus for the last fifty miles because the rental agency near the airport claimed to be out of cars. She wasn't used to that kind of treatment. At last, Tabitha knocked on the screen door of the cracker cottage owned by Meredith Lazar, third cousin to the reverend, who politely offered Tabitha a place on the couch in a room with screen windows. Meredith lowered the volume on the Philco. She put on her glasses with their librarian chain and got a look at the movie star of our group.

"Aren't you—" Tabitha prepared for her usual reply, 'Yes, I am. Thanks for being a fan,' complete with a bashful toss of her hair "—Willa Montgomery's niece?"

"Oh, uh, why yes." She was at a loss. "On my father's side."

It was her father's side of the family that gave Tabitha what in Hollywood was considered one of the loveliest tans on any starlet. Her pearly whites lit up the screens on road shows across the country as Isabel Radcliffe, the lovelorn entertainment hostess at a Caribbean resort community in *Conga! Conga!* Her smooth skin got teenage hearts racing as Jezebel "Jazz" Jacobs, an American spy who infiltrates the Kremlin, in the film based on the popular Broadway musical, *How I Spent My Summer as a Bolshevik*. Her dazzling eyes earned raves from even the harshest of film critics as Maggie Brogan, the Irish immigrant struggling to raise her four children and their darling puppy in *Bread Line Jungle*.

Tabitha had always been able to pass. Even in 1964, nearing thirty years in the business, she affected to perfection the presumption of admiration. How could those directors try to cast her as the grandmother? She wasn't old! How could her agent send her to a casting call for a television series? Tabitha swallowed a Valium with the Earl Grey offered by Meredith.

Despite a vague recollection of a distant relative said to be a church man, Meredith Lazar could only produce a filthy hat, some ragged shoes, and a worn cane that might have once belonged to Ike Zinnerman. Not a bit of documentation was on hand. Tabitha had finished half of her tea before realizing the peculiarity of the drink. June was at its peak. Mirages of heat could be distinguished through the screen window's pixilation of the world. Vapor from her cup made for an odd symmetry. In winter, Tabitha remembered, our husband would saucer his tea and slurp it like a dog. In summer, Tabitha remembered, our husband would ice it with cubes battered in sugar. Sweat began to melt her eye shadow.

On her way out the door, Tabitha saw fit to thank her hostess for such kind hospitality. Meredith asked her to say hey to her Aunt Montgomery. At the request, genuine as it was cordial, Tabitha, who had not spoken with her family since she left Mississippi almost thirty years back, who often told journalists she was born in Nebraska on a truck farm that grew strawberries, said, "Would if I could." She might have meant it.

"Woman is not a poet," Robert Graves wrote in *The White Goddess*. "She is either muse or she is nothing." Today, each of us having failed to solve the mysteries of our late husband, we wonder on the veracity of that claim. We are not poets. None of us even managed to succeed at the simple tasks we assigned ourselves. Forget that Mary Sue recalls Robert Johnson humming an unfamiliar tune around the house, mumbling the phrase, "Mississippi Mushaboom," as he wandered through the kitchen. Helena still would not have discovered his thirtieth song. Forget that Betty remembers having relations with a young man named Zinnerman, whose father not only had been lynched but also, the son said, had been completely illiterate. Tabitha still would have never found the last stanza to "Preaching Blues." What about the name of Robert Johnson's first child? We will never know. Across our individual lives, each of us failed not because of our own ineptitude, not due to our stupidity, carelessness, or misfortune, not because our goals were impossibly high, not even due to the intervention of fate and chance. We failed because none of us recognized the true mysteries of our husband. Not a one of us had yet found the other. That day would come soon enough.

PART THREE

CHAPTER SIX

Over the year following his recording sessions, beginning in Red Water, Texas, on June 28, 1937, and ending in Hoboken, New Jersey, on May 21, 1938, Robert Johnson traveled across the continent of North America. His friend boy Johnny Shines came along. Together they played Jitney Jungle parking lots in Tennessee and crossed dozens of raccoon bridges in South Carolina. Together they won a handful of simoleons at a dogfight in Illinois and bet on the Number Five horse at a track in Kentucky. They diluted the waters of Niagara Falls with their heavy piss. They christened the backyard at St. Andrew's Church of Toronto by squatting in the bushes. They fouled the bullpen of Wrigley Field with their thick vomit. Together they drove a forked eight through the countryside of Iowa, parking in cornfields for the night, swapping turns at the wheel during the day. Together they fell in with a group of tourists in the largest city of Ohio, wandering a brick path that ran beside the Cuyahoga River, looking through a viewfinder at the glassy expanse of Lake Erie. A postcard would have been nice.

Robert woke up coughing on a Saturday. It is unpleasant even for us to imagine it. Coughing yourself asleep is exactly like crying yourself asleep, and coughing yourself awake is exactly like crying yourself awake. We should know.

"Morning, sleepy head. Drink this down," Johnny said to

Robert, handing him a bottle of applejack. "You been sawing wood all night."

Our husband sat up from the floor of the apartment. Throughout the previous evening, he had patronized various saloons and consumed numerous pints of smoke, a variety of drink that cost a dime for a pitcher, its ingredients limited to stale beer, camphor, benzene, and malt residue. Not only did the applejack do the job of soothing Robert's understandably sore throat, but it also worked right fine at ridding his tongue of the smoke's understandably awful taste. Johnny stood across the room in front of a window. The view was a sight. Over to one side, a train on elevated tracks rained sparks onto the mane of a carriage horse, and to the other side, a smokestack puffed dark clouds over wet linen hung from a clothesline. The silhouette of a metropolis etched itself across the skyline. Outside the window—streets and alleyways turning into avenues and blocks, east side and downtown turning into uptown and west side—lay New York City.

"Where are they?" Robert said. "They still asleep?"

"In the bathroom."

"Time is it?"

"Quarter past seven in the a.m.," Johnny said. "Say we've got twenty minutes."

"Let's do the breakfast trick."

Without another word, both men found the electric icebox in the kitchen, removing enough food for a feast. Robert fried eggs and bacon on an iron skillet. Johnny boiled grits with cheese in a silver pot. They lathered toast with butter, squeezed fresh orange juice, and arranged two place settings. Twenty minutes from when they'd begun cooking the meal, steam rose above plates on the dining table, the eggs over easy, the bacon well done, the grits a tad burnt. Toast was piled high in the center of the table. Orange juice sat chilled in two glasses beside each plate. Robert and Johnny had only just closed the door to the apartment when two women emerged from the bathroom dressed for the day. Breakfast is, after all, the most important meal.

On their way through the lobby of the apartment building, known as the "Triple Nickel" due to its address of 555 Edgecombe Avenue, Robert and Johnny passed a mural depicting a scene from Greek mythology, Pan playing his flute to a herd of goats. Robert and Johnny walked down 160th past Broadway. Neither of them had a clue to their location, whether discernible by landmark or by neighborhood. They entered the Famous Washington Heights Diner, took a seat in a booth, and ordered the Polo Grounds Breakfast Special.

Johnny looked through the window and asked Robert, "Is that Brooklyn?" nodding towards the palisades of a nearby river.

"That's New Jersey."

"Like the cow?"

"Like the city in England."

"Is that a fact?"

They smiled at the custom of their own talk, how strong the bond was between them. Robert could be a husband to women, a companion, a lover, a caretaker, but he could only be a friend to men. Between sips of his coffee, black with two sugars, he asked Johnny, "What were their names again?"

"Hell if I know."

Last night, the sisters Barbara and Debbie Rollins, who worked as medical secretaries at Harlem Hospital in the wing kept solely for lungers, had invited the two bluesmen home from a bar called Plantation. They were the fourth pair of womenfolk Robert and Johnny had used for housing in just as many nights. Our husband didn't have relations with any of them. He swore it. We swear. He swore it. Oftentimes he played the women a lullaby song, but only 'til they went to sleep by themselves.

Next to him, Robert found yesterday's copy of the *Journal and American*, bulldog edition, its edges already going yellow from daylight. He offered Johnny, four years his junior, the funny pages. Robert was more partial to the classifieds. They gave him a sense of the city. The *Wanteds* and *For Sales*, with their roller skates size nine, with their golden retriever puppies, objectified it, and the *Personals* and *Services*, with their "Lonesome in Staten Island" signatures, with their "Learn the Piano in a Day" claims, subjectified it. All the details made New York a reality to our husband. Two plates of sausage-bacon-or-links and two-eggs-any-way and hash-browns-or-home-style rattled to quiet in front of Johnny and Robert.

"What you want to do today?" Johnny said, his knife and fork making ugly music against the stenciled ceramic. "Anything in the particular?"

"Don't know."

"Score me for a hundred. That was exactly my guess."

Over the past few days, Robert and Johnny had made a good many plans of things to do while in New York City. Eat corn dogs at Coney Island. Watch the White Star ships leave the docks at Chelsea piers. Buy a mango at the Washington Market. Chuck bread crumbs to the pigeons outside St. John the Divine. Since their arrival, however, Robert and Johnny had done nothing but drink, carouse, and sleep.

"Here's what I was thinking. We attend at one of them shows on the Broadway." Johnny's plate showed much little food left uneaten. "They say those dancers kick so high you sometimes get a shot of cooter."

Robert would have to think about that. On the newsprint, where his mug of coffee had left a ring, he noticed how the brown stain perfectly encircled an ad for services. The ad caused in him, he would tell us in other words, a will to solitude, the same sort of impulse, he would not tell us in any words, often felt in our company. Robert's next compulsion was to construct a newspaper hat.

"I was thinking we might go separate today," our husband said. "See what kind of trouble we can find on the split."

"What? Okay. Fine. Really?"

"Just for today. Something different. Meet up tonight."

"Bango."

Johnny was disappointed they wouldn't spend the day together. Robert could tell by the look on his friend's face that Johnny was disappointed they wouldn't spend the day together.

It took Robert all morning to reach 35-49 83rd Street. Above the door hung a plaque that read, "Establishment Owned and Operated by Burgess Hutchison," beneath, "The World's Greatest Teller of Fortunes." The only thing worse than having two last names was having the first of them be most common among people who were men. Burgess Hutchison had begun her fortune-telling career a decade earlier in Tulsa, Oklahoma, where she'd been taught by a Shawnee chieftain with a poor tendency to drink. "Best of my students by far. The Great Spirit was strong with her," he would later tell us after he had a few. "She was also fantastic in bed. Used to call her Wakes the Neighbors."

Burgess Hutchison left to ply her trade in New York. She picked the borough of Queens to set up shop owing to that's what she thought of herself. The predictions of the fortuneteller were as unreliable as her sanity. She told one of Dutch Schultz's runners that the Detroit Tigers would defeat the Chicago Cubs in game six of the 1935 World Series, but she also advised a German via telegram that the Hindenburg would be a nice way to make his transatlantic voyage to the States. She could prepare an excellent quiche when she wasn't conversing with oatmeal crème pies. During irregular intervals throughout the year, Miss Hutchison received her mail at Bellevue's "Observation" Ward, the only outcome of which was a phobia of electricity.

Her beauty would forever be the only constant in her life. She was Black Irish in a way. Her father was from Belfast and her mother was from Nairobi. Miss Hutchison's skin matched in both color and consistency her neighborhood's brownstones. She should have worn a brassiere under her housedress, but she instead chose to let the local boys get theirs. Her curly but pliable locks required neither comb nor pick. She had only two physical deformities. The second toes of her feet were a bit longer than her big toes. Just the thought of them disgusts us.

Robert pushed the button for 3A. It didn't take more than ten seconds for somebody to holler from a window for him to watch his head. Behind him too few feet away came the smash of metal on pavement. Robert retrieved from the sidewalk dozens of keys rung around a copper wire. He had no idea which of them would open the door. Whoever had told him to watch his head answered the question almost as soon as it entered his thoughts.

"X marks the spot!"

That the key stamped with an X slid smooth into the deadbolt lock gave Robert confidence in his decision to go it alone today. Somebody up there must have liked him. Inside the building, through the portcullis and porte-cochere out front, the lobby had mosaic tiles, a stamped-tin ceiling, and marble inlays; the stairwells, iron balustrades; the hallways, saw-tooth moldings and plaster walls and tongue-and-grooves. Flecks of glass sparkled beneath the varnish of wooden doors. Robert knocked on 3A. His last swing hit air. With one hand, Burgess Hutchison welcomed Robert into the apartment and, with the other, offered for a shake.

"No, honey," she said. "The keys."

"Sorry. Here."

Despite its ample square footage and lovely view of a garden, the apartment consisted of only one room, a head-scratcher to Robert in a number of ways. The bathtub squatted in the middle of the kitchen area. No bed was in sight. The toilet stood across from a large wall closet. One sink provided all services. The room had once been the servant quarters for an apartment owned by the Vanzetti family of Vanzetti Pasta Company, but it had since been converted to a studio in order to pay the tremendous debts accrued during the Flour Riots of 1837. All throughout Miss Hutchison's affordable home, the only light came from beeswax candles and paraffin lamps, some flickering upwards from spots on the floor, others hanging by shoestrings from the ceiling. The only sound came from the fortuneteller.

"Did you hear that? They're scurrying inside the walls. Afraid of the false light."

"Say what now?"

"They do it just to get up my rile. Damn heathen creatures. Did you bring the money?"

Robert gave her the twelve dollars they'd agreed to over the telephone. She put the bills down her top, blinding one eye of a bird dog. Miss Hutchison then commenced a whole to-do with nothing much to be done. She shuffled across the room, opened the closet door, and removed a folded cloth, and she shuffled back across the room, unfolded the cloth, and whipped it onto a table. Our husband watched Miss Hutchison's rump making all kinds of twitchwork against her thin, flowery dress as she placed two rickety, hard chairs opposite each other at the round café table. She asked him to take a seat. The session got underway in broken dose.

"What kind of a name is Burgess for a girl?"

"What kind of a name is Robert for a girl?"

He was attracted to her, we are repulsed to say. Did the touch of her hands on his palms remind him of the way Claudette would pull splinters from his pinkie toes after he'd walked across the porch drunk and barefoot? Did the rub of her ankle against his calf recall how Betty used to pinch the stamen from a honeysuckle and anoint his tongue with golden syrup? Burgess Hutchison studied the hands of Robert Johnson. She voiced the brilliant deduction that he played guitar.

"That's amazing." Too little irony sounded in his voice. "How'd you know?"

"I'm a certified psychic, honey." Her grin sure was full of teeth. "Like to know your future?"

"Only if it's good."

"Don't jest of the occult."

She chewed her own tobacco twice. He answered yes. With permission, Miss Hutchison removed a Major Arcana deck from the pocket of her dress and placed the tarot cards at the dead center of the table. She asked her client to cut the deck.

Even though the set-up always reminds us of a chestnut-bell, something we've heard before many times 'til now, the story of Robert's fortune picks up in excitement at the point when Miss Hutchison situated the cards in a spread known as the Celtic Cross. Five cards were placed on the table in the shape of a cross and another four were placed vertically beside the cross and one card was placed horizontally at the center of the cross. All ten cards of the spread represented the divination of our husband.

"Many blues artists from the Age of Freud claimed to have foreseen their own demise," *The Blues Almanack*, our primary source for this episode, states in a footnote, "but none conformed quite so well to the Freudian topology of their unconscious mind."

Miss Hutchison explained the cards to Robert. The spread portrayed the "Fool's Journey" of his whole entire life. On the first card, the bottom of the center, a picture of Judgment, an angel looking over mankind, meant that Robert's central question was one of forgiveness, and on the second card, the top of the center, a picture of Lovers, two people naked before a holy being, meant that the conditions surrounding his question were ones of relationships and choices. The latter card could also represent an aspect not yet considered of the former. On the third card, called The Emperor, a king sitting at his throne represented the hopes Robert had for himself, and on the fourth card, called The Empress, a queen sitting at her throne represented what Robert had experienced throughout his life. "That's the first I've seen of such a pairing," Miss Hutchison said. "Extraordinary women must be common to you." The fifth card, representing what has come in the past, was The Wheel of Fortune, a rotary with six spokes crested by an Egyptian sphinx, and the sixth card, representing what will come in the future, was Justice, the goddess Athena holding a scepter and a balance scale. "See how this Wheel of Fortune card is placed upside-down?" Miss Hutchison said. "Means your life has always wavered between chance and fate." The next three cards of Robert Johnson's fortune symbolized, respectively, his attitude towards his past and present, the influence of others in his life, and his hopes and fears for his future. The seventh card was The Fool. It depicted a young man, white rose in one hand, small dog by his side, walking towards a cliff. The eighth card was The Hanged Man. It depicted a person strung by their foot from a wooden beam. The ninth card was The Devil. It depicted its namesake, horned and winged, presiding over two naked human demons, a male and a female, both chained to his seat. "The tenth and final card is known as the Culmination Card," Miss Hutchison told Robert. "It's the end result of all the other nine cards." The card known as Death is oftentimes called The Trump with No Name. It depicts a skeleton riding a horse through crowds of dead or dying people. The skeleton outfitted in heavy steel armor carries a black flag emblazoned with a white rose, while the horse blinkered by leather flaps tramples the dead or dying bodies in its path. At sight of the card, the fortuneteller provided our late husband with two syllables as empathetic as they were heartfelt.

"Boo-hoo."

The day had sunk to gloam. Some people label such time the shank of the evening. In Miss Hutchison's former servant quarters—the yellow afternoon light going to shades of yellow, the vague flickers of candles turning to distinct flickers—Robert's stare moved its focus from the skeleton on the horse, to the toilet against a wall, to the bathtub in the kitchen, to the sweat on a brown neck. Burgess Hutchison stared at Robert Johnson and Robert Johnson stared at Burgess Hutchison. Each of their feet took refuge in places where feet don't belong. Robert got his throat clear so as to thank Miss Hutchison.

"Call me Lady Hutchison," Miss Hutchison said. "It's my essential name."

"Lady Hutchison."

"Mr. Johnson."

"Can I ask you one more question?" our husband said. "Do you mind if I ask you one more question?"

"All means."

"Where is your bed?"

At the first letter of the last word, removing her toes from his crotch and wiping the sweat from her clavicle, Miss Hutchison quickly stood from the table and walked towards the large closet doors. She pushed them open to reveal the backside of a mattress. She pulled a latch that read, "Murphy Wall Bed Company," until the contraption hit the floor. The fortuneteller grabbed her client by his collar, forced his body up from the seat, and guided him to an answer for his query, where in the dim light of paraffin lamps the two of them got personal with each other.

That poor woman, we believe, did not possess what it takes, believe us, to become a play pretty.

Although the pubic lice Burgess Hutchison gave him soon went away—please accept our sincerest thanks, Petty Officer Rick Jennings, for advising him of the naval cure—Robert could not seem to rid himself of the fortune she had told in such detail. His future haunted his present. Everywhere, walking along the esplanade in the shadow of the Brooklyn Bridge, buying a pint at one of the blind tigers on the Bowery, he discerned the vision of his own death. The drunks lying on stoops became in his mind bodies gone to rot. He saw the representation of his providence in the flora and fauna of city parks, those beady eyes of squirrels clambering up the trunks of oaks near Grant's Tomb, that piercing song of orioles hopping from branch to branch on the poplars around Sheep's Meadow. Hansom cabs sent him into fits of anxiety. Officers on mount led him to run for cover. He heard the symbolic version of himself not only in the laughter from audiences in moving-picture houses but also in the silence from greasepaint mime performers at subway stations. Critical looks from pushcart vendors made him awful weary at the stomach. On a particular occasion, Robert passed a three-story limestone house on the Upper West Side and, at sight of the gargoyle on the top ledge, scattered the pigeons on Columbus Avenue with the splatter of his sick.

Robert and Johnny spent the week following their initial separation doing to each his own. We like to think of them as two lightning bugs flying separate and alone during the light of day, only come dark to find themselves caught together in the child's jar of a dancehall groggery. They met early this one time. At Dickie Wells, a Negro Harlem gin mill on the part of 133rd Street known as the Jungle Alley, Robert and Johnny sat eating bagels, lox, and capers, an exotic delicacy to Southern boys on the make, as the saloonkeeper tossed handfuls of sawdust onto the damp floor. Sunset wasn't for an hour.

Across the table, Robert studied the face of his friend, noticing bits of soap curd dappling those buffoonish ears. He said, "Where'd you spend today?"

"Went to a bagnio near Tompkins Square," Johnny said. "Did you know a nickel extra gets you a bath?"

"Lean forward. I mean it. Turn this way."

Robert dipped the end of his necktie into a glass of beer and wiped the soap from Johnny's earlobes. He cleaned a smudge at the corner of his mouth.

"Seen any famous folks yet?" Johnny ran a sleeve over his chin. "Be a shame if not."

Ever since he first came to town, Robert had been hoping to spot some of the celebrities featured in the gossip gazettes and scandal sheets of a lower class than *Life*, *Vogue*, or *Look*. He kept a baseball in his back pocket, Claudette thinks, so he could get an autograph if, by chance, he ran into someone from Murderers' Row of the Yankees. He hid a flask in his coat pocket, Betty feels, so he could offer a nip if, one day, he saw somebody from the Vicious Circle at the Algonquin. Despite claiming his fanaticism as cause for seeking out the famous, Robert actually sought to analyze their behavior towards a public he felt he would soon have for himself.

"Nope," Robert said. "You?"

"Uh-uh," Johnny said. "None."

Our husband's arrogance might have proved justified if only he'd had more time on the flat side of earth. In December of 1938, seven months away, John Hammond, talent scout and music critic, arranged a production called "From Spirituals to Swing" to be held at Carnegie Hall. Not only were society's bluebloods to attend the black-tie affair but also film and radio stars. It is said Joe Louis had tickets. Although Robert Johnson was scheduled to perform on stage, he "died last week at the precise moment," Hammond inaccurately claimed, "when Vocalion scouts finally reached him and told him that he was booked to appear." The truth of it is John Hammond had already heard from Ernie Oertle that our husband was dead. No scouts ever came on his behalf.

"I'm going to get us something stronger to drink." Robert pushed his chair back. "I think that fish might have been raw."

At the bar, he asked the black man in a blacker apron for a fifth of rye and two glasses. That barkeep, Samuel Birdwell, eighteen years of age and obsessive-compulsive and with no formal education, had a photographic memory. He would later tell us in his penthouse at Harrah's in Atlantic City that he recognized the two men from the pictures we showed him. They had stayed in the bar most of the night. One of them took thirty-seven seconds to find the last nickel in his pocket to pay for a .75 liter bottle of rye. "Didn't tip neither." Birdwell considered three percent customary.

"How much this cost?" Johnny asked as Robert placed the bottle and glasses on the table and filled one with the other.

"Don't worry about it."

Johnny always thought himself the bad penny. We know

better. Two days back, Robert had been losing his shirt, probably still fragrant of the linseed soap from our wash buckets, at a stuss house in Brooklyn, while nine states away, we'd been struggling to feed his children, certainly never to know him by more than a hat on the bedpost, with nutria and mullet. Artistic temperament is not conducive to financial health.

On Johnny's question of how much money Robert had left to his name, for example, our husband told him, "I've got plenty," when the true answer was, "You're drinking it."

"How much *you* got left?" Robert asked Johnny.

"Gripsack's getting light."

"Nothing to worry about at all. I've got a line on something."

Johnny asked Robert, "What kind of something?"

Earlier in the day, our late husband told his best friend, Robert had been playing on a stoop near the Café Royal, trying to earn scratch, when a man wearing a yarmulke handed him a slip of paper. "You've got skills on that thing," the man said. "Call this number if you ever need a job." At first, Robert assumed the old man with the yarmulke was some kind of hallelujah peddler, but then he unfolded the canary onionskin to see the name and number for the "Hurricane Cove" saloon in Hoboken, New Jersey, a joint featuring "Real Dance and Live Music."

Robert took a first shot of the rye. "What do you think, Johnny?" He went into a short hacking fit that was unusual for someone with his experience at the bottle.

"What do I think? I think I'm sick of lying around loose. That's what I think."

"Bango."

Past sunset, Dickie Wells began to fill with its nightly patrons. A young man falling out of his breeches from lack of food could only manage to talk mush and molasses he was going drunk so fast. Ladies of various complexions sat in the corner, like brindle cats on a radiator, with a wishing book in each of their laps. An old man as grizzled as a gold-miner after a trip across the Rockies held an ear trumpet what better to hear the price of a drink he couldn't afford. Robert poured another shot as Johnny said, "I just got two concerns."

"Uh-huh."

"Where the hell is Hoboken and how the hell do we get there?"

Robert swallowed his rye and filled the other glass. "Always with the questions," he said. "You sound like my wife."

The next day, Robert and Johnny watched the sunrise at Dickie Wells and walked to the subway station on Lenox Avenue. They took the 7th Avenue Local on the IRT line down to the Christopher Street stop. It cost five cents. They took the New Jersey ferry from Christopher Street to the city of Hoboken. It cost four cents. They went up Washington Street and took a left on 3rd Street. At Hurricane Cove, twelve cents left between them, Robert and Johnny asked to see the man in charge.

Proprietor since the Treaty of Versailles brought our boys back to the States, Harold "Tidewater" Cutsworth, fifty-six, ran the saloon on Jefferson Avenue with one eye towards the old and another towards the new. Hurricane Cove was known as a place to be in New Jersey. Its business model was thoroughly modern—brown paper bags delivered to politicians and mob bosses, exclusive contracts with liquor companies and tobacco barons—but its atmosphere was decidedly archaic. Tidewater had first had the shiny chromium top of the bar dismantled and replaced with genuine eighteenth century mahogany. He'd had the electric lights replaced with gas wall-mounts. Tidewater had even run a shipment of slate shingles through an empty concrete mixer so they would appear sufficiently venerable lining the roof.

His rhyme and reason were partial to song and dance. Every night the center stage featured a musical performance fit to get the crowd shaking their things. Tidewater gained his appreciation for the "Call and Response" theatrics while growing up with his grandmother in the Low Country of South Carolina. The woman had Gullah blood in her veins. She taught her grandson their customs as well as their language. On Tidewater's Pinkerton card, the result of a stretch Out West during his rambunctious years, the list of unlawful infractions includes "Petty Theft" and "Simple Assault," but the list of distinguishing characteristics features only one item, "Trace Speech Patterns of Low Negroid Descent." The three-by-five card describes his intelligence as deceptive, cunning, and dangerous.

"Somebody outside de Cafe Royal, eh? Must ah been Lenny duh Finkelstein," Tidewater said on Robert and Johnny's answer to his question of how they'd heard of the Cove. "Jew friends they be good for de business. Did he look de wrinkly one-eye dinky in dat cap?"

Robert and Johnny didn't know whether to laugh or beg pardon. They were standing in the doorway of the saloon's back office, the owner reading a ledger of figures in a black walnut chair with red velvet, the accountant in a green celluloid eyeshade punching numbers at a corner desk. The adding machine struck a mighty racket. It distracted Robert and Johnny from deciphering the dialect, part Cajun, part Jamaican, part African, spoken by the man who'd introduced himself as Mr. Cutsworth.

"You twos won duh play de guitar for here place?"

"Yes sir," Robert said. "We do."

"What be dis about eight huned to de Looney bros?" He pointed at the ledger. "We done paid de Looney bros five huned usual."

The accountant said, "The Looney brothers said they want eight hundred from now on. Said the border patrol is getting tough."

"How about ten each per de night if you gwine play?"

"That's fine, sir," Johnny said. "Awful generous."

Tidewater asked if they owned tuxedoes. Johnny and Robert gave each other a dead pan that would have made Laurel and Hardy proud. Tidewater said that would not be a problem. He asked if they would they excuse him for a moment.

Twenty-five seconds later, Tidewater stood in the doorway of Hurricane Cove clenching a baseball bat. On the sidewalk crouched the accountant. His hands were clasped together in beg of mercy, and his face was washed in red by a deep laceration. From the windows gawked the bar customers. Tidewater screamed, "You tink you can steal fum me?!" before his second at-bat.

On their way back inside, Tidewater turned to the stone faces of Robert and Johnny, apologized again, and said it had been long coming for Zachary Obadiah Matthews, the accountant, whose name never relents in tripping our tongues. He guided them through the bar. A shack that Tidewater called the "Praise House" stood on the plot of land directly behind Hurricane Cove. The Praise House had been the former residence of the unfortunate Zach Matthews. It contained a large king bed, three Shaker chairs, a potbelly stove, two Regulator clocks, and a closet full of numerous, colorful suits and four identical tuxedoes.

"De clocks are for you twos to always be on time," Tidewater said as he walked out the door. "De accountant not gwine be needing his tuxedoes no moe."

Robert and Johnny settled into the Praise House. They took to their arrangement with ease. On the first night, they played to a crowd that filled roughly half the table space of the saloon. Johnny Shines wasn't just some nanny goat to Robert Johnson's thoroughbred. He could hold his own. The two of them began to accord with each other better than either of them had ever known possible. On the third night, they played to a full house with a line of people waiting all the way down the block. Tidewater started to charge a cover for Hurricane Cove and doubled the wage for both Robert and Johnny. The line grew longer. From the bar men ordered cocktails, Old-Fashioneds and Sazeracs and Rusty Nails, while on the floor their dates tried the latest dance, the Lindy Hop or Trucking or the Susie Q. Blues listened good. Despite Johnny's talent, not to mention his ability to strike an impressive pose on stage, there was no question which pretty little brown thing all those people came to watch. Our husband must have looked handsome in his tuxedo. We take solace that bowties cannot be hung proper from a doorknob.

On the eighth night, Robert and Johnny, both having saved over $100 since they'd begun, took to the stage only to discover a room empty save for two women. Who should be sitting at the front table but none other than the sisters what a few weeks ago had provided the bluesmen a place to stay the night.

Debbie and Barbara Rollins had bought every available ticket for that night's performance at Hurricane Cove. They told Robert and Johnny how much time it took to track them down. They asked Robert and Johnny what happened that morning two weeks ago. Lies come easy to some men.

"We're so damn sorry we didn't send word. How could y'all afford this whole place? It's so damn good to see the both of you."

The sisters were rich according to our research. Rumor had it that in the spring of 1929 their father, then Joseph Kennedy's favorite shoe-shine boy but later a man on Wall Street in his own right, warned the famous stock-market investor to watch his ass. William Rollins eventually established Rollins Mutual. The joys of his life were said to be his two little girls. They were all he had left after their mother died during the flu outbreak. For those reasons, it worried him day and night that Debbie and Barbara, rather than live a life of leisure he would gladly have provided for, chose to work at Harlem Hospital in the tuberculosis ward. His apprehensions were as solid as his investments. In late October of the following year, Barbara would be dead from complications due to her line of work. Debbie would last 'til Thanksgiving.

At Hurricane Cove, Robert and Johnny gave the sisters their money's worth. How the strings of those guitars did twang. The first set went an hour, the second an hour and a half. Afterwards, Barbara and Debbie gave a standing ovation and asked the bluesmen back to their hotel room. Our husband pulled his partner aside.

"I'm not going with y'all."

"Why not?"

"Can't burn a barn twice."

We think even once is too much for a barn. Where would you store the hay? What about the plow? Where would you stable the horses? Metaphor can be as unreliable as euphemism. Barns can go to hell.

Robert said this wasn't just for tonight but for good and all. Johnny seemed to take it pretty well.

"How am I to get home?" he asked.

"No one ever showed me the way."

Without even a handshake goodbye, Robert left his friend alone on the dance floor with Debbie and Barbara Rollins. He took off his tuxedo in the Praise House and changed into his own clothes from Mississippi. He knocked at the door of the back office and waited to be told it was okay to enter. All he got was a low grunt.

Tidewater sat leaning strutwise in the black walnut chair, lacing a coin through short fingers. He said, "What canee do for oonuh, Bob?"

"Giving my notice. Tonight's my last night."

"Bob duh blueman say he gwine to be quitting my joint." Tidewater looked towards whatever the Gullah took to be their lord and savior. "Dis after I provide Bob duh blueman with de shelter, de food, de money."

"Johnny will stay on long as you need him."

Tidewater fixed his gaze on Robert. He lifted his arms up high and put his hands behind his head, revealing a shoulder holster and the butt of a Savage .32 ACP. "Johnny he be good on de guitar playing, but people dey ain't coming to see him." The gunmetal caught the overhead light.

"Then you can take this for all your trouble. Should cover my absence for a while now." Robert tossed a $100 bill on the desk prior to walking away from it. At the door, no longer thinking of his death in spite of the firepower two yards away, he turned back and said, "At least keep Johnny on for a couple more days."

In September, four months later, the Great Hurricane of 1938 would make landfall on Long Island, sending seventy-five mph winds down Bleecker Street, flooding the East River up to 2nd Avenue, but on May 21, Robert Johnson prepared to leave Hurricane Cove, stuffing his suits into a duffel bag, pocketing his last thirty dollars to the penny, slinging his guitar case across his back. Rambling was no longer on his mind. He coughed into the barrel of his fist, got his bearings to Hoboken Terminal by studying the traffic, coughed into the white of a hankie, took a Delaware, Lackawanna & Eastern train on the cut-off line, coughed into the cuff of his shirt sleeve, and had to walk from Memphis Union Station south towards home, only then noticing that his fist, the hankie, his sleeve were smeared by SOCONY-Vacuum Oil axle grease, damp from sweat, blotchy with Hudson River Co. kiln-brick soot, and freckled in blood.

“Me and the Devil Blues”

Over the years—even as some of us found hope in 1960s radicalism, even as some of us found stardom in 1950s Hollywood, even as some of us found oblivion in 1970s decadence—our lives settled into the insignificance of routine and lapsed into the quotidian of womanhood. We married men whose features should have been those of our first husband, and we gave birth to children whose last names should have been that of our first love. We scrubbed dishes until our hands shriveled unrecognizable. We mopped floors until our faces warped in reflection. We washed laundry with Our Lady Umbrage™ Detergent, and we dried laundry with Sovereign Flowers® Fabric Softener. In those stretches of time, days passing into weeks, months passing into years, we all believed our true identities as the wives of Robert Johnson and as the keepers of his secrets had never been discovered by the various writers and journalists of the publishing industry. We believed the biographers, magazine editors, and newspapermen, so many of whom had begun to chronicle the history of blues music, did not know of our existence. We were wrong.

What about the blues, we have wondered at times, so draws people to harness it into words and sentences and paragraphs and chapters? Literature and music, two art forms seemingly at odds with one another, can no more coexist within the same medium than the sun and moon can light the same sky, than fact and fiction can illuminate the same subject. Perhaps the very impossibility of the task gives siren to writers of a certain steadfast ilk. Perhaps literary ambition, like our search for the truth of Robert Johnson's life and death, must set her sights for the unattainable, the incomprehensible, the irrational, the unforgettable.

One such ambitious writer tricked two of us into betraying the secrets of our mutual husband. In the 1960s, while living in Chicago, Helena became involved with the civil-rights and anti-war movements. She hummed along to Mahalia Jackson's rendition of "Take My Hand, Precious Lord" at Martin Luther King's funeral. She picketed in protest of the Kent State Shootings. She patted James Meredith's back as he crossed the racial threshold of Ole Miss. Although her husband, who wrote crosswords for the *Tribune*, owned a three-bedroom apartment in Oak Park, Helena spent most of her days on Chicago's South Side, where the local youth advocacy group kept their headquarters. The Children of the Revolution, as they were known, maintained distant but substantial ties with the Black Panthers and the Merry Pranksters. Not only did Helena tell them which books to study, quoting Thoreau and Angelou in lectures as fervent as they were erudite, she also advised them on what streets to march and at what venues to hold sit-ins. To the Children of the Revolution Helena was known simply as "Godmother."

Even though she was just over fifty years old, Helena still caused traffic to lurch into gridlock every time she crossed the street. Her beauty was a pothole. One revolutionary child, a young man who'd joined the group just a few weeks prior, took particular notice of Helena. Derringer Swope, which he claimed was his name but which we think smacked of artifice, looked in every way the trust-fund intellectual. His Windsor glasses glinting their low prescriptions, his henna tattoo flexing on a thin tricep, and his facial hair trying in vain to fill a beard, all traits so earnest yet so pathetic, somehow endeared him to Helena. One day, after weeks of casual eye contact that was anything but, Derringer Swope approached her. "Godmother, I hear you're originally from the heart of the heart of the Delta," he said. "Must've been like the back nine of hell. I'd love to hear about it sometime." We do not blame Helena for succumbing to the charms of a goateed, tattooed, bespectacled incubus. Nor do we blame Helena for taking the young man home with her on the night her husband was out of town. Crossword puzzles have always bored us.

During the night, as she tried but failed to sleep sound, Helena grew increasingly aware of odd inconsistencies from their earlier conversation. He had claimed to be from Alabama, but he possessed no hint of an accent. He had said he'd never heard of Robinsonville, but he immediately asked about Son House and his crew. His questions raised her suspicions. "What were the economics of sharecropping?" "Have you ever heard about Alan Lomax's theory of cantometrics?" "How often did you travel on Highway 61?" In the morning, even before she opened her eyes, Helena knew the young man's body would no longer be lying by her side. Seconds later, as she opened her chest of drawers, she knew also that her diary would be gone.

At various times over the years, the same man has come in contact with each of us. We do not know how he caught our scent. We do not know how he followed our trail. In Dallas, he knocked on Claudette's door, dressed in the creased slacks and wrinkled shirt of a city worker, inquiring if he could check the meter in the basement. Claudette asked for credentials, but he could not provide them. In Los Angeles, he found Tabitha's table at the Brown Derby, saying he was on profile assignment for *Photoplay*, a yellow pencil pushed behind his ear, a white press card stuck in his fedora. Tabitha checked with the publication, but they had never heard of a reporter by his name. In New York, he disguised himself as a homeless vagrant and rifled through the discarded mail in Mary Sue's curbside trashcans. The police scoured her 5th Avenue residence within a three-block radius, but all they found was a pile of panhandler clothes purchased from a downtown theatre company's prop sale.

Despite our overall resistance to his attempts, the young man of polymorphic appearance was able to hoodwink one more of us into spilling secrets about Robert Johnson. In the 1970s, while living in various towns throughout the Delta, Betty pursued a long-term career as a drunk, each juke joint, flophouse, and pool hall serving as her office. She would sleep one off at the Pink Pony Café in Darling. She would tie one on at Booba Burns' Place in Greenville. On the night she encountered the young man recurrent to our lives, Betty was tossing back pints one, two, three and chasing them with shots four, five, six at The Playboy Club No. 2 in Louise, Mississippi. Along the walls hung signs for Schlitz Malt Liquor, "No One Does It Like The Bull," and for King Cobra, "Don't Let The Smooth Taste Fool You." A constellation of iridescent bug zappers hung from a ceiling with no light fixtures. Window curtains were draped on a wall with no windows. A folding chair in the bathroom sat over a toilet with no plumbing.

The young man, whose glasses were Wayfarers instead of Windsors, whose face was five-o'clock shadowed instead of goateed, and whose skin was inked with a dozen designs instead of just one, sat next to Betty at the bar. Once the bartender had explained their pricing system—all whiskey is seventy-five cents, all ice is twenty-five cents, all cups are fifty cents each—the man turned to Betty and said, "That's where they get you. The ice and the cup." Betty told him she drinks straight from the source and raised a bottle of Green Label to her lips.

The young man, after offering to buy her next round, told Betty his name was Madison Malone. If she'd had her senses about her, Betty might have questioned, as the rest of us did, the veracity of such a name. If she were but a half-bottle less drunk, Betty might have found it odd, as the rest of us did, for a white man to buy her a drink at The Playboy Club No. 2 in Louise, Mississippi. They clinked Dixie cups in cheers. They struck their Lucky Strikes. They tapped the timber for more tipple. At the backside of midnight, after Betty had admitted to having known Robert Johnson, after she described his music, his personality, and his looks, after she told stories formerly known to us and only us, the young man stood from the bar. He tossed a twenty on the checkerboard counter, taking a step back into the bug zappers' neon gloom. Just as he began to make for the door, Betty asked the young man why he wanted to know so much about a bluesman been dead for forty years. He told her, "I'm writing a book, Missus Johnson," as an electric melody dropped a diminuendo of flies to the floor. The young man walked out of the bar at the same moment Betty's unconscious face pawned the checkerboard, her cheek smushing against the black and white squares.

On August 23, 1982, *The Blues Almanack* by Wilson Smatterhorn—only a man with a name so ridiculous could have invented "Derringer Swope" and "Madison Malone"—was published to critical acclaim. It stayed on the *New York Times* Bestseller List for twelve weeks. The most comprehensive examination of the history of blues music, *The Blues Almanack* contains entries on everyone from Muddy Waters to B.B. King, from the Rolling Stones to the Mississippi Sheiks. The longest chapter in the book chronicles the life and death of Robert Johnson. Among the historical facts, oral anecdotes, and hypothetical conjectures that comprise the chapter, we recognized information stolen from our encoded diaries and extensive archives, from our crumpled letters and drunken talk. We saw ourselves hidden between the lines. We heard our voices transmuted on the page. Yet not once did the author reveal his source. Not once did he acknowledge the chorus of women who, just as years ago we did for our mutual husband, provided inspiration for his work. Neither Wilson Smatterhorn nor Robert Johnson ever thanked us in public or in private for performing our duties as muse. All these years we have waited for his gratitude from the grave. We wait still.

CHAPTER SEVEN

Our husband could not get shed of his competitors. On Catfish Alley in Columbus, Mississippi, a curbside venue that had in years past brought him a hat full of change, Robert was surrounded by a whole mess of homegrown musical acts, a harmonica palmer and a tap dancer and a bucket drummer. His guitar case, empty but for the starter nickel at its belly, lay open next to a puddle of crankshaft oil, and his duffel bag, shut tight beneath a coat of red dirt, held a fresh sack of hotfoot powder. Our husband was tempted to use the powder on the other musicians. Rheum in his eyes, wax in his ears, and phlegm in his throat, he had a tough job at seeing the strings, at hearing his chords, at singing the song. Robert could not keep up with the Joneses. It was time to find a doctor.

Between Dublin, Philadelphia, Cleveland, and Rome—Mississippi cities are metropolitan by proxy of nomenclature—he had been getting worse for wear each day of travel. Not once did he send word. Robert gathered his things up in his arms, tipped his hat in surrender of the territory, and went in search of the local physician. August was coming fast. Everybody's garden held too many tomatoes. On his way across town, passing the Christian Church on 6th Street, not even noticing the Mississippi State College for Women except for its water founts, passing the Friendship Cemetery on 13th Avenue, Robert felt as though he were in a temperature dream. We imagine he could almost hear the Columbus townspeople of 1863 serenading Jefferson Davis outside the Whitfield Mansion with their songs of freedom from national oppression. Governor James Whitfield's residence in Columbus had been modeled after President Thomas Jefferson's home in Monticello. Robert Johnson would have ignored such an otherworldly tonal coloration emanating from the ideologically dialectic construction now called the Billups Home. He kept on.

At the outskirts of Northside, the colored-folk part of town, our husband, spitting a loogie of red on the ground, wiping a booger of green from his eyes, discerned a sign that declared, "Bernard Chesapeake, MD," the snakes of its caduceus writhing in Robert's feverish perception. So help us he was sick. The low roof and red frame of Dr. Chesapeake's office lay in the shadow of an umbrella chinaberry tree. Inside was cooler. The secretary told Robert it would be ten minutes before the doctor could see him, but she led Robert out of the waiting area and into the check-up room after only five.

Dr. Chesapeake sat at a desk across the room, his white-jacketed back facing Robert. "Take a seat over on yon examination table," the doctor said as he scribbled in a book. "Be with you in three shakes of a moment."

Considerable taker of notation, crosser of sevens, slasher of zeros, and thorough questioner of patients, Dr. Chesapeake scrutinized Robert, asking his name, date of birth, place of birth, shoe size, waist size, height, political-party affiliation, astrological sign, residence, profession, and marital status. The smell of his breath, subject to the confluence of Tennessee brightleaf and Kentucky sour mash despite the midday hour, could primp an eyelash.

We will not say the doctor was drunk. Southerners are never drunk. They are drinking or they are not drinking.

The good doctor had been drinking a while. He scooted over in his non-rolling chair and said, "Now tell me where it hurts," a mercury thermometer hanging from his mouth.

"My chest and my throat and head most all," Robert said, making half a Sign of the Cross by touching each. "Everything aches something bad. I can hardly hear. My voice is weak. Eyes are blurry. And sometimes, uh, when I cough, uh, there's blood."

Dr. Chesapeake clicked his pen and wrote a few words in a folder. He removed the thermometer from his mouth, tapped it against his lips, and slipped it into the front pocket of his shirt. He muffled a belch.

"You can tell me, Doc. Is it the consumption?"

"How am I supposed to know?" That was not what our husband was expecting to hear. "I'll tell you how. Instruments!"

Across the room, Dr. Chesapeake searched a black leather satchel for what seemed most a lifetime. He returned to Robert with purpose. The doctor placed the cup of a stethoscope against his patient's chest and told him to take a deep breath, but the other half of the instrument still hung around the doctor's neck rather than in his ears. "Interesting." The doctor placed his fingers against the patient's carotid and counted his pulse for sixty seconds, but the wrist at which the doctor stared the whole time had plenty of freckles though nary a watch. Dr. Chesapeake said, "I think I see the problem," looking around the room.

He again searched through his medical bag. Out the window he could only find sunflowers staring their petals back at him, and under the desk he could only find slut's wool huddling in the corner. He came back to Robert with less purpose.

"It seems I've lost my thermometer," Dr. Chesapeake said. "But I have a diagnosis for you."

"Okay."

"You do not have consumption. That is for certain." The doctor's voice had to fight against the volume of our husband's sigh. "It's a touch of pneumonia, heightened by exhaustion. How long have you had the symptoms?"

"About two months."

"There you go. Should have come see me much sooner. I've got just the thing." Dr. Chesapeake handed Robert a bottle of Mother Superior's Elixir. "It's a miracle tonic. Will cure anything. Pneumonia, the flu, exhaustion, chilblains. Take two gulps twice a day."

"Will do."

The doctor pointlessly told our husband to see him again the following week. "Do not, I repeat, do not," he said as Robert got to the door, "play or sing for at least a month."

In the waiting area, paying the secretary four dollars for the session and two for the bottle of miracle tonic, Robert could have sworn he heard from behind the check-up room's door the especial sound pork rinds and egg yolks make as they splash against the bottom of a sterile waste bin.

He took a swig of Mother Superior straight from the bottle and left the office of Dr. Chesapeake forever and all. The time of day was nigh past noon. At the intersection of 14th Avenue and Moss Street, the devil started to beat his wife with a frying pan, both sun and rain colluding to yield steam from the hot pavement. The Lowndes County sky had sealed back up by the time Robert neared the banks of the Luxapalila River. He wrangled his way through a thicket of japonicas, boxwood, and gardenias, stumbling onto the oddest prospect he could recollect of late.

Take our hats if it wasn't an oaklimb baptism. Throughout the shallow waters of the Luxapalila, townspeople, black and white, young and old, stood half-leg high in a semi-circle, each of them wearing only but a croaker sack. Their clothes were piled in a heap on the shore. At the center of the semi-circle, a man wearing a black suit with the sleeves rolled up dipped the townspeople gradually but certainly into the water, one of his hands holding their necks, the other holding their noses. The man gave proclamations after each. Our husband could not make out the man's features with any reliability, so he drew quiet footfall across the patchwork crabgrass towards the river. That was when things took a turn for the strange. The man sure did look damn familiar, his height excessive of eighteen hands, that dark skin, those bright eyes, his weight insufficient of fourteen stone, but it could not possibly be him. Robert got respite to his wonderment and trepidation when the man locked stares with him, gave leave of his congregation, and waded to the shoreline.

"Reverend Ike?"

"Hello, Robert."

That was the second and last ghost Robert Johnson would encounter over the remaining days of his life.

Although they had been born fraternal twins, Herman and Ike Zinnerman were mistaken all their lives for identical. Not only strangers confused their names but also kinfolk. Appearances were deceptive. Contrary to his brother, the reprobate, the profligate, Herman, whose birth certificate specifies he exited the womb second, could read all twelve Disciples' names in Braille, train a bird dog in less than a fortnight, and paint da Vinci's *The Last Supper* without numeral guides. What is most curious is that two brothers who as children behaved so differently—Ike playing five-card monte on street corners, Herman carving burlwood into religious icons—would both choose, albeit one legitimately and the other counterfeitly, to be jackleg preachers.

Ever since they'd left home at age seventeen, one heading for the *Dixieland Queen III* docked on the coast, the other looking for the Colored Baptist Association way up north, Herman never once heard from Ike until he received word of his death. He had to postpone a prairie burial in order to process the news. How could his brother wind up hung from a tree in the front yard of a whorehouse? Herman never fully believed in the death until one afternoon, washing away the sin of Columbus Christians in the brown water of a river, he noticed standing along its bank the last man to see Ike alive.

"So you heard I was with him at the end," Robert said to Herman, both of them sitting on a log of floodwood beneath a shade tree next to the river, "but how'd you recognize me just now?"

"Saw you play in Vicksburg couple years ago. Didn't yet have the fortitude to confront you then."

Above their heads in the dark of cypress canopy, a spider hanging on its line drifted in rhythm to the gummy river breeze, a pendulum with the world for a clock. The spider clamored back up to its web in the tree, stopping time in mid-tick of a hot summer afternoon. On the dry bank, Herman's congregation exchanged their croaker sacks for clothing articles, all of them as brazen as Adam and Eve before the taste of fruit. Nary an echo reckoned with their movement. Along the current of the river, invisible water bugs skimmed its calm surface, their wake the only way to know they were there. Herman said, "Can you tell me anything about how he died?"

"There's a story, but I'd rather not."

"I understand. He was your friend."

"Did so much for me before what happened happened," Robert said, situating a cigarette. "Guess I owe him more than I'll ever know."

He patted his pockets. Herman gave him a packet of matches, the box white, the stick white, the head white. On each of the preacher's knuckles, Robert noticed as he lit his cigarette, were two different tattoos, "Dismas" and "Gestas." Our husband had never heard of the terms. He tried to give Herman back the matches.

"Keep 'em."

"What's with the ink on your fists?"

"There's a story," Herman said, "but I'd rather not."

That got a smile. Between drags of his cigarette, Robert administered his second dose of Mother Superior, already feeling the lull of "eleven mystical ingredients from the far reaches of the globe" in his throat and head. He coughed once, but it didn't hurt.

"Your brother was a very good man."

"My brother was a complicated man."

Cruel, stupid men have cruel, stupid brethren. The same is true for the opposite. Yet, whereas Herman put his generosity of spirit on display for all the world, Ike kept his own hidden behind the gift of a remarkable intelligence. Both were confidence men in a way. One professed myth as truth while the other told lies as legend. We consider the key difference between the two brothers to be that one of them genuinely believed in his own falsehood. A man must be complicated to sell religion, but a man must be goddamn crazy to buy it. If Herman Zinnerman weren't black, mark our words, he would have spent time in a white room at Whitfield.

Needless to say we are not very religious. Neither was Robert. So, when Herman asked, "Since you're here, Robert, I feel obliged to ask if I could baptize you, given certain talk I've heard tell of your talents," our husband responded he would only put a toe in the Luxapalila come hell or high water.

"That's what I feared you'd say," Herman said. "It's never too late to accept Christ."

"To be completely on the up and up with you, I honestly can't imagine a God who would forgive someone like me. There's certain things I can never forgive Him for neither."

"Many have faced similar dilemmas," Herman said. "Could I ask how old you are now?"

On July 3, 1971, Jim Morrison, twenty-seven, mistook heroin for cocaine while sitting in the bath at his Paris apartment. The medical examiner claimed to have found no evidence of foul play. On October 4, 1970, Janis Joplin, twenty-seven, threw up while laying on her back on the floor of a room at the Landmark Motor Hotel. Her last recording was a birthday song for John Lennon called "Happy Trails." On April 5, 1994, Kurt Cobain, twenty-seven, put a double shotgun to his forehead at his Lake Washington home. A note was found stating he hadn't felt excitement while creating music for too many years. On September 18, 1970, Jimi Hendrix, twenty-seven, took one too many sips of red wine at his girlfriend's flat in London. His manager was said to have been very upset because the musician had wanted to end their contract. On July 25, 1938, Robert Johnson, soon to be considered a charter member of what became known as the Forever Twenty-Seven Club, told Herman Zinnerman, "I don't know."

"Christ was thirty-three when he gave his life for our sins."

"The young will always be a foolish bunch."

Herman's arms fell loose as though he were on the nod. His face grew red as a dragon's placenta on display in a museum. He kept his mouth shut. His eyes went the way of a bucket risen fresh from a well house in spring. Only a man with empathy as big as prison could end up so locked inside himself. Stubborn, frustrating, obstinate, mean, hurtful, sly, arrogant, and irascible, Robert could also be selfless, kind, respectable, warm, childish, trustworthy, delightful, and virtuous. A wife knows. It wasn't that Robert disliked Herman for any logical reason. Despite all evidence to the contrary, Robert still, deep low down, took the twin brother of his old friend, sounding as Ike had sounded, looking as Ike had looked, for a revenant.

"I'm sorry you feel that way," Herman said, hitching aloft from the driftwood. "It was a pleasure making your acquaintance."

"It was nice meeting you likewise. We should catch up another time."

Men always lie in clichés—"I swear to God," "It meant nothing," "You are the only one," "I love you"—especially to other men. Herman gave Robert some help standing with

Dismas and patted him on the shoulder with Gestas. The two of them wandered away from the river. At the edge of city limits, bullfrogs ribbiting from the shore behind, box turtles rustling through the grass ahead, Herman asked Robert if he were looking for work on the guitar. Our husband told him always.

"Over in Greenwood there's a regular dance they give every Saturday night. I pass through there quite a lot in my travels. They're always looking for good six-stringers to give the people relief from their toils. Does that sound like the kind of work you might like?"

Robert Johnson said, "Course," to Herman Zinnerman. We would like to say little did he know, but the truth is little did any of us know.

CHAPTER EIGHT

Greenwood, Mississippi, kept up more compresses, gins, and warehouses than any Delta town our husband had ever had the pleasure. Cotton was regal. Naught but hardly a vantage could be taken without seeing some speckle of white in the lands outlying the city proper. At a quarter 'til eleven in the morning on a Friday, Robert walked down the street known as Boulevard, home to planters and merchants made wealthy by those same compresses, gins, and warehouses, the while humming a cheerful tune despite his poor condition. He took a gulp of miracle tonic. Although the doctor had warned him against playing until he was well, Robert had aims for working the country dance Herman Zinnerman had recommended back in Columbus. He so easily could have come home and taken rest in any one of our beds. What are wives for if not to tend their men well? He instead meant to risk everything for to play a night of blues music. Church folk will put it all on the next life. Robert put it all on this one.

He had some time to kill before he was set to audition for a store owner at five. People on the streets in the white part of town seemed anxious at his presence, owing either to the color of his skin or to market season having just begun—it takes from August to late December for cotton prices to stabilize—so Robert decided to tour the fringe of Negro quarters surrounding the other business and residential districts. Back then Greenwood had seven Negro sections. Burkhalter's Alley and New Town were small, no more than twenty houses or so, but Gritney, the oldest and largest, occupied near to thirty acres. G.P. Town could be found south of the railroad tracks. Ram-Cat Alley was home to the best cooks. Buckeye Quarters got its name from the oil mill. In Baptist Town, where at the time Robert sauntered down a sidewalk of newly poured concrete and where years later we were unable avoid a crack while tracing his steps, the church spire at the section's center could obviously be understood for its namesake. The sign, "Now Entering a Certified Main Street Community," would be erected when, decades hence, the neighborhood underwent "G.I. Bill Gentrification."

On passing a mailbox printed with the name Shaeffer, Robert halted in the manner of a cold jaw given a violent jerk of the reins. Somewhere a woman was singing an old spiritual. Our husband daren't say it came from the backyard. Along the side of the house ran a dirt alleyway strung on both sides with picket fences a foot higher than a man. Robert walked down the alleyway until he came to sound level with the woman. He had a breeze of luck in that a knot of wood made for a hole in the fence, its circumference just about wide enough to bear his good eye for sight. Lo to behold. On the other side of the fence, hanging sheets from a loose clothesline and sweating from the heat of a dog day, stood what even we own was a mite beautiful creature. She could not have been more than three times ten years old. Her smooth and supple flesh was the light brown of a sunshot fetlock. Her tantalizing face and features were a testament to all mavenhood. Once she'd put the last clip on the sheets, the woman leaned over a heavy bucket of water, dipped her hands in it, and swathed herself from temple to thigh, causing her nipples to materialize beneath her white dress and her behind to take shape by clinging at the fabric. Robert held his potato.

Her kiss-curls glistened blackly as she walked deeper into the yard. She left view. Robert began to scuttle and sidestep at the canter of a crawfish, each foot behind the other, never a once taking his eyes from the wooden planks of the picket fence. His technique proved unfortunate. Farther down the line, Robert, whether overwhelmed or merely whelmed, did not notice that the fence came to an end, its purpose replaced in part by undergrowth pocked with trumpet creepers. Disaster was on the make. At the juncture of wood and brush, Robert fell into the nettles heel over head, rolling forward in his effort to stand. He lastly gained a purchase when he was full in the backyard. The young woman gasped at the intruder. She covered herself with a sheet. Only after Robert had managed to stand up straight, dusting himself off with the brim of his hat, did the woman gather at his appearance, pull her lips into a smile, and proclaim, "You scared me."

Our husband had been to Greenwood a time or two before that day.

Later in the afternoon, Robert Johnson lay atop a feather mattress with Regina Shaeffer, spooning crank ice cream between them, while far in the distance clarion bells sang the toll of heaven's gate. The chimes came from the courthouse. Every hour on the hour, they would set forth unto Greenwood a melody written to the lines, "Lord, through this hour be thou our guide, so by thy power no foot shall slide," the tones in duplication to those of Westminster in London. Robert gave another melting spoonful to Regina. The two of them made sweat angels on top of the sheets. They'd been hurried in it without letup for on about two hours. "Lord, through this hour be thou our guide," the bell went again, "so by thy power no foot shall slide." With his tongue, still tasting the unguent of nethers, Robert caught a dribble of vanilla at Regina's chin.

"I think you get prettier every time I see you," he said, a classic from his catalog. "What barrel have you been drinking from anyway?"

"It's been two years. Imagine you can't even remember how I used to look. We'll see in two more."

"You hush up now."

"Can't say I'm complaining at the sweetness, though," she said, running the needle of a finger down the turntable of his chest. "Harold but never gives me that kind of—"

"What time is it, honey?"

Robert knew from the number of bell dongs that, afternoon on its haunches, the time was just past four, as well as that, given he still worked at the cotton-oil mill, Regina's husband would be home soon. At the answer to his question, "It's only four, lover, so we got time," Robert told Regina that he had an appointment at five, that it was awful nice seeing her, that he would probably be in town at least a couple weeks. Some women will believe anything. It astounds us.

On his way to Three Forks, a small division of acreage three miles east of Greenwood at the intersection of Highways 49 and 82, Robert hitched a ride on a Hoover cart, that old-time type of two-wheel lolly, idling past tupelo gums, grain elevators, snuff signs, rained-under corn, burnt-out corn, duckweed, phlox, verbena, blue swamps, yellow swamps, green swamps, and a prop ag plane. All of us can remember such ephemera of the former world as clearly as Betty, the drunk, remembers the smell of our husband's hangovers, as easily as Mary Sue, the rich one, remembers the sight of our husband's wallet, as gently as Claudette, the archivist, remembers the feel of our husband's fingerprints. Have mercy it was such the long time ago. Robert got to the country grab-all store just in time for his audition, only to have its name send him feeling as the wrong end of a donkey. *Could it be the one and same?* he asked himself.

Shaeffer's was built in a style known as Southern Shack. Its sloping roof of deeply corrugated tin sheets and its gallery across a weather-beaten front contrasted the stately pediments of good second-growth pine stuck every two yards across its slat porch, whereas its one-story frame, mud-wattle chimney, and wide but long, sway-back portico testified to the sparseness of its interior layout and the fingernail moon cut into the door of its outhouse. We disremember the rest of its structure. The building would be razed soon after our only visit.

Despite his cautious footfall across the yard, Robert's arrival was heralded by the cry of rusted hinges on the store's screen door, but no greeting fell his way. Hog-killing time had come early for the grab-all. Beneath the plate glass of the meat display were piled maple-cured hams and mesquite-smoked sausages of all girth. Backbone, spareribs, and chit'lings lay under a cake bell in a sideboard by the dry goods. At the butcher table behind the counter stood a man grinding hogshead cheese. Must have been a cold snap of late. Robert said, "Evening."

The man reeled around from back like a carnival fright dummy on springloads, his cleaver raised high at the ready, his eyes indicating murderous intent. "Jiminy Christmas! You scared me about half to death," he said, putting down the knife and letting out his wind. "I'm sorry about the blade. Shoot! What can I do for you?" The man hit near to five-five in thick socks, weighed on the cheap end of a buck-fifty, and wore the spats and stays of a farm-come-town dandy. His shortish fingers were delicate as snap peas. The man could be said to be all ears, literally and figuratively, as they were the size of philodendrons.

"I'm here about the dance audition. Robert Johnson. I'm a guitar picker by trade."

"Think I've heard the name. Mine's Harold Shaeffer."

Robert could only cough in response.

"We run a tight operation round here, Mr. Johnson. People expect the best. Can you play on a close level to the best?"

"Yes, sir."

In a corner behind the counter sat an old-style wireless playing at low volume. Robert got tickled pink as a peony when "Terraplane Blues" came on the air. The track, staticky but discernible, played all the way through rotation as Harold, affable and chatty, explained how every Saturday he held a country dance in the space behind the grab-all. He spoke of how his usual clientele included tenant farmers and the like. He mentioned his high sales of corn whiskey as well as his fondness of live music. He explained that each staff member, musicians to servers to barkeeps, got a portion of the profits. "Terraplane Blues" ended at "fifteen percent."

"Supposed there's only one thing left to discuss," Harold said. "Would it be a problem to hear some of your music?"

"No problem at all." Robert pointed at the wireless and said with his smile of a piece, "You just did."

It took Harold a second. He stared at the wireless, rubbed his chin in a facsimile of clever, and chuckled after some thought. "Knew I'd heard the name." Harold's open hand struck Robert at the shoulder. "You got the job." On his offer, Harold spit into his palm still slimy with hog meat and pushed it towards Robert, who wasted less than no time at all in returning the favor. Harold asked Robert, "Have you got a place to stay?" without wiping his hand.

"Figured I'll find a roomkeep somewhere in town."

"We've got a spare for let in my house. The missus can make a tasty cobbler. Regina loves company. What do you say, Mr. Johnson?"

God—he thought—*damn*. Robert pondered on the matter while looking slaunchways through the window. The night was coming to dark pretty good. It would be terribly difficult to get back to town without help of the flatbed pickup sitting out front of the store. Our husband figured what the hell.

"I think I'll take you up on that one," he said. "What's the worse that could happen?"

In the summer of 1974, years after the two weeks Robert Johnson spent in his house, years after the slow realization Robert Johnson was sleeping with his wife, Harold Shaeffer, our husband's murderer, would be seen for the last time at a fishing camp near Key West, Florida.

On Saturday, August 13, 1938, Robert was set to play the country dance at Shaeffer's in Three Forks, his second performance at the venue. Word had gotten out. Old plantations in Mississippi have colorful names—Hard Cash, Arrowhead, Need More, Duck Pond, Island, Egypt, Christmas, Better Day, Wildwood—not to mention all manner of colorful workers. The Star of the West plantation, one of the largest in the state, provided Shaeffer's, one of the commissaries for the place, with most of its customers. Damn near all showed up for Robert. Due to the time of year in the crop cycle, the rest of the audience was on break from the Buckeye Cotton Oil Mill, Federal Compress and Warehouse, Planters Oil Mill Gin, and Staple Cooperative Association Warehouse. The dance on this particular night had drawn its biggest crowd yet. Over 200 country and city folk piled into the back lot of Shaeffer's.

Our husband felt worse than he could recall, throat itchy, breathing painful, talking painful, chest heavy, but he managed to procure relief elsewhere. God takes care of two types of men, and Lord knows Robert wasn't a fool. His miracle tonic had long run out. Behind the bar, he sat on a cane-bottom chair, sipping at moonshine and conversing with Craphouse Bea, one of the waitresses for the dance.

At sixty-four years old, Craphouse Bea, with her former good looks, with her low tolerance for sass, with her stylish gold tooth, reminded Robert of Callie Craft. Perhaps that was why they enjoyed each other's company so much. Bea asked Robert, "Did I tell you about the time I found a fellow making the love to one of those horses out back?"

"Nah."

"He looks at me looking at him and says she may not be the prettiest thing, he says, but he always enjoyed a woman who knew how to take a carrot."

Robert had a good one at that, so much so his hankie got red. He quickly hid it from sight. At the same time, though Robert didn't notice, Craphouse Bea was staring across the room at Harold Shaeffer, who stared fiercely back and shook his unctuous head. The old waitress said she had to go tease a cat with a long stick.

On her way to the outhouse, according to witnesses from that evening, Bea made as though she were stifling tears. Damp hiccoughs could be heard at twenty yards. We have never been certain how we feel about her. Helena, the activist, thinks she was an innocent but gullible woman forced to felony by a pathetic coward, whereas Tabitha, the starlet, thinks she was a corrupt fraud who faked a conscience to hide her guilt and complicity. All we will ever truly know is what she did to our husband. We suppose that is more than enough.

Katydids foretelling dusk and mules braying in their stalls rent the momentary quiet as Craphouse Bea came back to the dance and composed herself at the wagon sheet. Robert started his first set as she traversed the crowd. At the bar, Bea gathered a tray of splo whiskey in shot glasses to sell for a nickel each, the Onkoi mask of her face all the time switching between comedy and tragedy. She would smile for a moment, and she would frown for a moment. Jokes for one patron would come right after insults for another. She would dance to the music, and she would stand still to the music. On the stage, conversely, Robert appeared the singular spectacle of a bluesman, those hands that needed the pluck of a string as begonias need a Charleston trellis, those lips that hung on the poetry of lyrics as children hang on their Nehi bottles.

Who could have known he was bound for the other side?

Surely not the audience. They pretty near danced themselves fat. The only person who could have known what was to occur was the same person who could feel the final disease already taking hold. Robert sang so hard and so raw and so loud that flecks of blood sprayed on his strings and shoes. Calluses flowered to blisters until blisters withered to pouches. Across the room, in plain sight of Robert on center stage, Harold Shaeffer gave a glass of whiskey to Craphouse Bea, a devious gaze passing between the two conspirators. Robert did not stop in his music.

You ask us, he saw them. Our husband knew the grave was close by means of one of two routes. Beneath the cathedral glow of strung oil lamps, Robert's eyes moved in step to the glint of Bea's gold tooth as it took passage from the bar, through the crowd, and to the stage. His song was now over. She fetched Robert the whiskey, saying, "It'll plenty light a shuck," to which he thanked her.

Years of five-cent tobacco and 100-proof liquor had eroded Robert's taste buds as certainly as too much rain in June or July will wash away topsoil. He therefore did not notice that the whiskey, itself of rough flavor, had been doctored with a lethal dose of passagreen, a type of strychnine, its taste said to be akin to battery acid. Passagreen is made by boiling moth balls in vinegar. It was a cruel joke that Shaeffer's wife, along with many women of the era, often used passagreen as a douche. Robert took a slug of his drink, and his world became kingdom come.

The first effects of the poison had as much influence on our husband as they did on the entire audience. That his voice became an unearthly wail and his playing sped to an inhuman pace did nothing but to send the people into convulsions much like those of a church revival. All throughout Robert Johnson's very last song, "Love in Vain," the audience went into the "moaning fits" and "praying shouts" of the Holy Dance, raising their arms to the heavens and shutting their eyes to the world as they "came through experience." Men pulled their hair from the root and swallowed it with a chaser of beer. Women ripped their dresses at the seam and exposed their bosoms to the night. The music lived in their minds long after its sound had died. Craphouse Bea had already vanished with Harold Shaeffer.

During the crowd's religious rapture, our husband, muscle spasms breaking his vertebrae and bowels turning loose their contents, crawled along the ground, brushing against pants with the cloth eaten at the knee, stumbling over boots with heels worn to the nub, bumping into legs full of veins from long hours, until he entered the sandy loam-soil acres of The Star of the West. Nobody gave notice. They were still dancing. They were still dancing in a place that had gone silent.

Robert Johnson was pronounced dead three days later despite the absence of a body. According to the State of Mississippi death certificate, the place of death was accurately listed as "County: Leflore" and "City: Greenwood (Outside)," but the date of death was inaccurately listed as "8-16-'38." The principal cause of death was left completely blank. The section for contributing factors contained only the phrase, "No Doctor."

On his arrival in Greenwood, Herman Zinnerman, who when he heard the news felt unbearable guilt for sending Robert towards his death, took it on himself to investigate the matter. He heard conflicting versions of the event. What he was told more or less by townsfolk present at the dance corroborated more or less with what we have come to believe more or less actually took place. The other versions, however, brought on doubt.

Some said our husband did not die from the poison. They said the combination of whiskey and sickness had sent him into such a poorly state he had to be carried off the stage on an old piece of cotton cloth. Tush Hog, a moniker given to any tough person and therefore useless in identifying the man, put Robert Johnson on the back of a wagon and drove him to a rooming house in Baptist Town. There he was laid up for rest. During his convalescence, Zinnerman was told by a woman named Eskridge, Robert got so feverish he began addressing his nurse as "Mother." He told his mother the guitar was the devil's instrument, cursed the day he ever took it for work, and begged her absolution in the ways of his life. Soon thereafter he succumbed to pneumonia.

Others said our husband fell ill due to complications from syphilis. On the back of the death certificate, a note written by the Leflore County Registrar states that Robert was taken to a white man's house on The Star of the West plantation, where he was believed to have been syphilitic and eventually died of the disease. No evident foul play in the death meant there would be no murder investigation. According to the cotton pickers, choppers, packers, and haulers, each of whom Zinnerman questioned in detail, Robert Johnson did indeed die at the big house and he in fact wrote a last note from his deathbed. The note resides in our collection. "Jesus of Nazareth, King of Jerusalem," it reads, "I know that my Redeemer liveth and that He will call me from the Grave." The handwriting does not match that of our husband.

All throughout his inquiries into the death, Zinnerman could never get the straight of how Robert had passed away. Zinnerman got the closest to discovering the truth when he visited the site of Robert's last performance. Shaeffer's was boarded up window to door to window because, common word took it for gospel, Harold and his wife had left town soon after the death. Zinnerman coerced his way in with a crowbar and rummaged the storage room of Shaeffer's. Among haphazard trinkets from over the years, including wadded Juicy Fruit wrappers, ignition switches, Remington .22 short cartridges, and St. Joseph Aspirin, he found a guitar with an X carved into its back and a medicine bottle that smelt of a bad woman's toilet. He also found an empty tin of mustard shine for throwing bloodhounds off the track of shoes.

That was far as Zinnerman would ever get. He saw to it that our husband as embodied by his guitar was funeralized big, its head directed to the west rather than crossways with the world, so as he wouldn't have to turn around to rise when Gabriel blew his trumpet. Despite such efforts for a Christian burial, the Greenwood townspeople had begun spreading the rumor that Robert's body was never found because Papa Legba had sprinkled it with a devilish quicklime. That was why Zinnerman forged the deathbed note. He did not want our husband's memory tarnished by the very legend that would ultimately sustain it.

Over fifty years later, at his home in a city he asked us not to disclose, Herman Zinnerman would say, "I got there just two days too late. At the time I asked the Lord to forgive me. Now I know there is no such thing."

We have never been certain if he meant the Lord or

forgiveness. Our husband's death elicits the same uncertainty. Did he die of poison given to him by a jealous cuckold? Was he taken alive to Baptist Town only to die of pneumonia? Would he possibly have written the deathbed request for salvation? Could his mother really have been present in spiritual form at the end? Did he curse the instrument that made him famous? It does not matter. He is dead. We are alive.

"Kind Hearted Woman Blues"

What can we say of what can't be said? During the years following Robert Johnson's death, our separate lives plagued by so many things we could not express for our mutual husband, the only way to survive was to try to forget the need. Distraction was paramount. We filled pear halves with mayonnaise. We killed plantar warts with duct tape. We ridded gardens of snails by placing bowls of beer on the ground, cut brown felt into patterns for school pageantry, and resisted the urge to dangle sundry items in front of cats. We made ours with Miracle Whip. We took coffee Irish on bad mornings, forced the children to study Latin to better their chances for a good school, and said it was all Greek to neutral therapists. We dated hippies who frequented the VFW and married bankers on leave from the Peace Corps. We lined our Medicare pills on the bedside table and filled a tall glass with cool Evian water. We rubbed our thumbs against the bristles of a toothbrush, yelled upstairs they did not feel wet, and waited for voices that had left the house decades ago. We watched soaps. We darned rags. We trimmed nails. The comings and goings of seasons came and went until the prime of our lives had come and gone.

Only as old women were we able to find the words. At the Blackjack Church built in a famous sweet spot of Mississippi hill country, where two legendary music thoroughfares,

Highway 16 and Highway 51, meet to form a crossroads of some renown, an event was held to celebrate the life and times of Robert Johnson. 2001 was called Year of the Blues. On the day of the event, all of us still under the delusion that each of us was his one and only, we arrived in a range of automobiles, Lexus and Civic and Chevy and Limo and Buick, the fields of skip-row cotton on every side of the parking lot a tribute to the majesty of a land we had long forgotten. Each of us carried flyers—"Biography of a Phantom: The Influence of Robert Johnson on Modernity"—along with cans of bug spray. Not everything was beautiful return.

The title of the event was borrowed from a book supposedly being written by Mack McCormick, a folklorist who claimed to know so many secrets regarding our husband that his would be the definitive text on the musician, but enough decades had lapsed that now Mack McCormick claimed the book would not be ready in his lifetime. We climbed the gray steps of the Blackjack Church, named for a type of oak in its vicinity, passing through walls of red brick trimmed in white mortar. The audience was highly diverse. College students sat next to tractor drivers sat next to music teachers sat next to lawyers sat next to doctors sat next to housewives sat next to children sat next to hill farmers. Those pews of glossy oak had not carried such a mix of race, profession, and age since the church was founded in the early part of last century.

Patrons of the statewide Mississippi Blues Festival sure were putting on the dog. From the rafters throughout the church hung banners depicting the face of our late husband. Men in dark suits handed out programs with a list of the speakers. From the Peavey amplifiers on the walls came an elevator rendition of "Cross Road Blues." A child with an open fly ushered people to their seats. We took ours.

At a flux of the overhead lights, similar to an extravagant theater warning the end of intermission, the entire audience settled into stillness and got busy getting quiet. The local county preacher, one of those youngish biblical handsomes taking over the church in this new age, approached the podium. Our programs had it that Pastor Ezekiel Thompson, "an amateur blues historian," would begin the celebration with a sermon. He would follow it by introducing the scholars and experts sitting in rows to both sides behind him. On his first utterance, thanks be to good fortune what with the venue, Pastor Thompson's voice exemplified more holy tone than holy whine, allowing for a pitch not unlike a traveling man.

The pastor began by saying that all we had left of Robert Johnson was twenty-nine songs, a death certificate, two photographs, and a false legend. He asked if everyone there that day had heard of Robert Johnson's bargain for his soul at the crossroads. "I humbly beg of you not to believe it. Stories such as those only serve to dehumanize the godliest aspect of mankind—art—because it is through music and other artistic mediums that we create. What is faith but the creation of belief?" He went on to say that Robert Johnson was faithful in God Almighty as well as in love. Not only was he a wonderful artist of blues music, claimed the pastor, but also a wonderful family man, a father, husband, and brother. Such words put us in mind of a quote from someone else.

"Women, to Robert, were like motel or hotel rooms: even if he used them repeatedly he left them where he found them. Robert was like a sailor—with one exception: a sailor has a girl in every port but Robert had a woman in every town," Johnny Shines wrote in the issue of *American Folk Music Occasional* from 1970. "Heaven help him, he was not discriminating—probably a bit like Christ. He loved them all—the old, young, thin, fat, and the short. They were all alike to Robert."

In conclusion the pastor told a story that took place at the turn of last century, a time of injustice, superstition, and poverty that would eventually give rise to blues music. The story concerned what was then called the Negro Question. "Someone asked a white landlord if his black tenants had souls. 'If the Negro does not have a soul,' answered the landlord, 'it's the first thing that a white man had that a Negro didn't share, if they stayed together for enough time.'" The pastor said he wanted everyone in the audience to understand that Robert Johnson proved that ignorant landlord both right and wrong. Our husband had a soul, he said, but chose not to share it. To end his sermon the pastor gave praise to Jesus.

We lost religion long ago. At the conclusion of the pastor's speech, therefore, all of us found ourselves surprised to witness so many people in the audience dabbing tears from their eyes. What a crock. Each of us, Mary Sue and Tabitha and Claudette and Betty and Helena, studied their faces. We saw in them an appreciation and an adoration we too once felt. Our hearts beat at 78 rpm, our lives are self-titled, and our natures have a B-side, yet our grooves are scratchy, our vinyl is warped, and our spindles are oblong. Therein lay the difference in us from them. Only we had been changed by love for him. Over the next few hours, though, we began to notice certain similarities.

During the formal presentation, as historians expounded on Robert's mysterious life and death, as musicians glorified

Robert's abilities with a guitar, as academics pontificated on Robert's cultural significance, our ears went deaf to their panegyric. All six of us continued studying the audience. In the fourth row from the back, a woman sitting apart from everyone else, half her face hidden behind sunglasses, worried at the hook of her diamond earrings. On the far right, a woman whose thick spectacles dangled from a chain and whose suit of hair frizzed around a clip scribbled ferociously in a marbled notebook. A woman at the dead center of the church space, symbolic ribbon on one lapel, political button on the other, could not find a comfortable place for her feet. On the far left, a woman with a misstep in her lipstick, panty hose overrun, and a black eye under make-up set her puffy jaw shut. In the second row from the front, a woman dressed in prim fabric with nice hems and coiffed near to statuary raised her eyebrows into an unnaturally smooth forehead. All the women, staring at the banners with his picture, seemed to hope to be asked for justice from Robert Johnson's eyes, but they also, glancing at their ring fingers, seemed hesitant to answer him with the penitence of their own. The look from each of their faces revealed a terrible truth. It's possible to lose one's soul to, for, and in the act of loving another.

We thought of what they say about misery. At the event's conclusion, three hours after its start, the young pastor once again took the high podium, the warp and woof of his demeanor unraveled by the length of the presentations. Ezekiel Thompson asked everyone to bow their heads for the Lord's Prayer. "Our Father, which art in heaven," he began, "hallowed be thy name." We could hardly listen to him, our minds were in such tumult. Yet sound was not the only sense kept well far at bay. Light from the stained glass windows pigmented our faces with various shade. We did not see it. Pressure from the hardwood of the pews forced the nerves in our legs to tingle with pricks. We did not feel it. Sweat from the people around us whiffed across our noses along each draft. We did not smell it. Dry air with each pull of breath spoiled the flavors on our thick tongues. We did not taste it. Only later would the sensations come back to us.

At the end of the prayer, just seconds having gone past, we heard those two words, spoken in a hush by the pastor, addressed to He who has possession over Judgment Day. We can hear them now. The words have forever become a part of our minds, not in reference to evil, but as a salve to our memories of a bluesman. Deliver us.

ACKNOWLEDGMENTS

Although *Play Pretty Blues* is a work of fiction, it required a great deal of research, particularly concerning the life of Robert Johnson. I'd be remiss not to mention Peter Guralnick's *Searching for Robert Johnson*, Elijah Wald's *Escaping the Delta: Robert Johnson and the Invention of the Blues*, and Barry Lee Pearson and Bill McCulloch's *Robert Johnson: Lost and Found*, books that were invaluable to the writing of this one. For historical context the WPA Guides to Mississippi, Alabama, and New York City were also helpful.

Thank you to all my wonderful teachers and fellow students at Columbia University's School of the Arts. I'm grateful to the members of my writing group, Tom Treanor, Abby Caran Griffith, Kimberly King Parsons, and Wendy Flanagan, who, throughout the time it took to write this novel, helped make every sentence better. Y'all are the tops. Thank you to everyone at Engine Books, especially my editor, Victoria Barrett, whose advice, insights, and judgment never failed to amaze.

I owe gratitude more individualized than is possible here to all the family and friends who provided me with their generous support over the years. Most importantly, I'm thankful to my parents, Charles and Becky Wright. Without them I would not be a writer. This book is their fault.

ABOUT THE AUTHOR

Snowden Wright was born and raised in Mississippi. He has written for *The Atlantic, Salon, Esquire,* and the *New York Daily News.* A graduate of Dartmouth College and Columbia University, Wright lives in New York. This is his first novel.